The Last Thunderegg

By L. J. Louden

Cover art by A.J.A. Louden

ISBN 0-7414-5825-X

Printed in the United States of America

This is a work of fiction. Names, characters, places, and incidents either are the product of the author's imagination or are used fictitiously. Any resemblance to actual events or locales or persons, living or dead, is entirely coincidental.

Published October 2010

INFINITY PUBLISHING
1094 New DeHaven Street, Suite 100
West Conshohocken, PA 19428-2713
Toll-free (877) BUY BOOK
Local Phone (610) 941-9999
Fax (610) 941-9959
Info@buybooksontheweb.com
www.buybooksontheweb.com

To my children -

Adrian, Anthony & Sara

Thank you for the joy and pride that you bring to my life.

“Somewhere over the rainbow, skies are blue,
and the dreams that you dare to dream really do come true.”

- Lyman Frank Baum

Chapter 1

Andy stuffed the money back into his pocket and grinned. He had just enough to buy the gemstone. It was rough, dull grey and oblong in shape. And it fit perfectly into his closed fist.

"Why do you want *that* one, Andy?" asked his mom. She had a smile on her face and pulled his ear as she poked another rock into his belly to tickle him. "Look at this one."

It was smooth, very polished, and green.

At least this one wasn't pink, thought Andy. "Nope," he scrunched his nose up at his mom and crossed his arms.

She laughed and ruffled his wavy hair. "Oh, you! I don't know what you see in that ugly thing. But, it's your money." Shrugging, she wandered down the aisle looking at the myriad of different stones on display.

He didn't know why he liked it, either. It just felt right. When he held other rocks, all he felt was a cold, hard stone. But when he dug *his* gemstone out from under the pile in the basket, it was warm. It felt like it was pulsing in his hand. And he was sure he saw faint flashes of color when the light hit it just right. Andy felt an immediate attachment to it and wouldn't consider trading it for any other stone. With it clutched in his hand, he continued to look through the other baskets.

Mr. Marley, the Banff Rock & Gem Store owner, kept glancing at him. He would watch Andy closely when his mom tried to convince him to spend his money on a *prettier* rock. Every time Andy refused to consider one his mom showed him, the corner of Mr. Marley's mouth would twitch and his eyes would twinkle.

Twelve year old Andy was small for his age. Long eyelashes framed his dark blue eyes and a splattering of freckles danced across his nose. He constantly battled with a crushing shyness and pronounced stutter.

When his dad died five years ago, his world turned upside down. They moved several times since then. Every move meant a new school for Andy. He gave up trying to make friends since the combination of his extreme shyness and stutter made him the brunt of cruel jokes. While quiet and withdrawn at school, when he was at home, Andy and his mom had a great time. They had a special bond – *the two of them against the world* – kind of thing.

Six months ago, his mom married Brian. Andy's new stepfather always had a smile on his face and never made any comments about his stutter. On the rare occasion that Andy said anything more than one syllable to him, Brian would just wait patiently for him to finish talking. And then he'd continue the conversation as if nothing was different. But Andy was still shy and uncomfortable around him. He didn't know what he should call him – 'Brian', 'sir', 'Mr. Crandall'? It just didn't feel right to call him 'dad'.

They left their home in Saskatoon, Saskatchewan for a two week summer holiday through Alberta and British Columbia. Andy had been excited for weeks and was impatient for the day they would leave home and start their vacation. They were going to camp in the mountains and swim in the ocean. Brian promised they'd go salmon fishing and build sand castles on the beach. And they'd brought their ball and gloves with them. The plan was that Andy's pitching arm would be so strong by the fall that the local teams would be fighting to have him as their pitcher. Andy wasn't sure how that was going to happen since all the kids told him he couldn't hit an elephant. But it was exciting to think that he might actually be good at something. And Brian could be such a goof. They usually ended up on the ground, gasping for air from the giggles.

The drive across the prairies was pretty boring. But the day they spent at the Calgary Stampede was full of rides and games, junk food and checking out the many barns housing lamas, sheep, cows and Andy's favorite, the horses.

As they left Calgary and drove west, all three passengers in the car became more excited. The Rocky Mountains - having a war with towering rain clouds as to which one would dominate the view - grew larger and eventually surrounded them as they followed the highway towards the renowned mountain village of Banff.

Chapter 2

The Banff Gondola Ride at Sulphur Mountain was the first stop. After climbing into their private glass paneled car, they stood - noses pressed to the glass - and watched as a panoramic view slowly materialized as they climbed. Snow capped mountains spread out before them. The higher they climbed, the more mountain peaks rolled into view.

Andy's mom turned - face beaming, "Andy, isn't this incredible?" Her expression quickly turned to one of concern when she saw him sitting on the floor, face slowly turning an odd shade of green. "Andy! Are you okay?"

"Uhhhhh.....uh,uh."

Brian turned at the sound of Andy's moaning response. "Uh oh. Are you afraid of heights, Andy?"

Andy peeked outside and looked down. His answering groan was all they needed to hear. His mom convinced him to breathe deeply and count to himself. Brian sat beside him the rest of the way up - insisting he keep his head between his knees. Andy, eyes closed, listened to Brian's silly jokes and stories, knowing it was supposed to distract him from his very nauseous stomach. When they finally reached the summit, he couldn't get out of the gondola fast enough.

"Geez, I didn't know you were afraid of heights, Andy," his mom ruffled his hair.

"Yeah, n-n-neither did I!" Andy's humor returned when his stomach stopped doing somersaults. "I sure d-d-don't want to go on that th-th-thing again."

When his mom's grin slowly disappeared - replaced by a growing look of concern, Andy's heart flipped. He suddenly realized that they had to get *down* the mountain.

"No! M-m-mom!"

"Uh, Brian…" his mom turned to her husband, at a loss as to what to do.

Brian grinned good naturedly. "Well, I guess we'll just have to toss you down."

Andy's mom raised her eyebrows in surprise.

"Or we could ask that bear over there to give you a ride down." He pointed to a neighboring mountain where a large black bear was meandering across a meadow.

Andy's jaw dropped. His mom's eyebrows lowered over her eyes as she glared at Brian.

"Or, we could walk down that trail over there," he pointed under the gondola to a well worn path that zigzagged down the mountain.

Andy's mom gave her husband a good natured slap on the arm while Andy heaved a sigh of relief.

Andy loved Banff. Wild elk wandered the streets and grazed in the meadows along the highway. Old, chalet style houses were nestled behind treed yards on side streets called Rabbit, Fox, Otter and Marmot. Tourists speaking German, French, Spanish and the occasional American twang crowded the busy sidewalks. Sports stores and souvenir shops stood shoulder to shoulder all along the main street. Candy was purchased by the pound at Welch's Candy Store and small crowds of people - mouths watering - watched fudge being made through a plate glass window at The

Fudgery. The fresh, crisp mountain air smelled of pine boughs at Christmas and newly mowed grass. He couldn't help but take big breaths - filling his lungs and slowly letting the air escape - eyes closed in delight.

When they reached the Banff Rock & Gem Store, Andy squeezed through the people coming and going through the front door. Once inside, he stopped and stared in awe. There were shelves and shelves of rocks. Every color, shape, size and texture that you could imagine. Baskets lining the walls overflowed with all sorts of different kinds of rocks. Most of them were polished until they were as smooth as glass. Others looked like they had been cut in half. One side was rough and dull looking. The cut side of the rock was hollowed out with hundreds of tiny brilliant purple, blue or white square chunks of color all jumbled together. There were glass cases holding necklaces and bracelets made out of tiny sparkling stones. By the front door, narrow rocks, almost as tall as Brian, stood at attention.

Andy had vacation money that his mom had given him - just enough to buy one of the small rocks in the baskets along the floor. After looking through several piles, he finally found *his* rock.

He was wandering through the store, captivated by the world of shining, colored gemstones when his mom interrupted his browsing.

"Honey, we're going to look at some more stores. Do you want to come?"

"Uhhhh…," Andy hesitated.

"You can stay here if you'd like. We'll only be gone for about half an hour," she said.

Andy nodded in agreement. He wanted to see the rest of the store. And he would keep his head down so he wouldn't have to talk to anyone.

"And you know not to leave the store, right Andy?" She nudged him, eyebrows raised.

Andy nodded again.

"What was that, honey?" his mom asked softly.

"Y-y-y-yes mom," Andy whispered, glancing behind him to see if anyone had heard him. He received a juicy kiss on his cheek which was immediately rubbed off with a disgusted, "Awww, mom!"

After Brian and his mom left the store, Andy pulled the hood of his sweater over his head, stuck his hands in the front pouch and slowly went from case to case inspecting their contents. There were rocks called *'Tourmaline'*, *'Amethyst'*, *'Amber'*, *'Quartz'*, *'Crystals'*, and *'Chalcedony'*. He wanted to know what his rock was called, so he picked up a book from one of the racks and started leafing through the pages. Apparently, most gemstones had some kind of power or mystical qualities. Crystals were thought to have healing powers and were used to tell the future. The amethyst was supposed to bring good fortune in war and drive out evil spirits.

He didn't find any rocks in the book that looked like the one in his hand. Returning to the basket where he found it, Andy kneeled down and started to dig. After a thorough inspection, he decided - with a mixture of pride and confusion - that he had a *one of a kind.*

Andy had been deep in thought, wondering about the uniqueness of his rock when, all of sudden, he realized the store was quiet. When he had come through the front door, it was full of people. There had been a constant buzz of talking, laughing, '*oohs*' and '*aahs*'. Now, it was so quiet you could hear a pin drop. He spun around and looked at the deserted store.

Mr. Marley - the only other person there - was watching him. The store owner was an odd looking fellow. His too long and tousled hair was all sorts of shades of grey. In contrast, his mustache and beard were neatly trimmed and combed. He wore a black beret - like the French painters. His old fashioned suit had a gold pocket watch tucked into the vest. Mr. Marley's eyes looked like they were black, but if the sunlight hit them just right, you could see they were a deep emerald green. *Mr. W. Marley* was printed in fancy, swirly letters on his name tag.

He slowly approached Andy, hands clasped in front of him. "All gemstones have names and special qualities," he began. His voice was soft and gentle. "For instançe, this one," Mr. Marley picked up a shiny black rock from a pile in a box, "is called a tourmaline. It's said to dispel fear and grief. According to legend, the tourmaline protects the wearer against dangers and misfortune. And this one," he picked up a sparkling pale green stone, "is called a Peridot. It's used to help dreams become reality."

Mr. Marley peered at Andy over his wire rimmed glasses and raised his eyebrows as if waiting for a response. When Andy just blinked, the old man turned and continued on down the row of shelves. Picking up a sample from each basket, he would give a brief description of the stone and then gently place it back where it belonged.

They had wandered to the back corner of the store - beside the basket where Andy had found his rock - when Mr. Marley's mood changed.

"Now, that one that you're holding is called a Thunde-regg," Mr. Marley's voice had become deeper, quieter and very serious. He gazed into Andy's eyes.

"It's very powerful and trjeklirnkvnenldanshahd fklgjseoirgfeioj…………………"

All of a sudden, some very strange things happened. Mr. Marley's words became garbled. Andy saw a flash of green out of the corner of his eye and heard a giggle. But when he glanced over his shoulder towards the baskets, there was nothing there. He brought his attention back to the old man. Andy shook his head but still couldn't make sense of what Mr. Marley was saying. The old man kept motioning towards Andy's Thunderegg and went into some kind of long explanation. Bending down so he was nose to nose with Andy, Mr. Marley's face had lost all signs of humor, his bushy eyebrows lowered over his eyes. It seemed like he was asking him a question, but Andy still couldn't understand him. He felt himself nod his head, but had no idea what he was agreeing to. He looked down at his Thunderegg and gasped when he saw it sparkle - ever so faintly - as if it was winking at him. Then, sensing a presence between the shelves again, he glanced over as Mr. Marley straightened up. He thought he saw something.... Or did he? The air between two of the baskets had a greenish hue. And objects in the area looked a bit distorted. Andy blinked and everything was clear again. Even more confused, he brought his attention back to Mr. Marley.

"So, your journey begins." Mr. Marley's voice was back to normal. The tall man straightened and clasped his hands in front of him. "That Thunderegg has chosen you to ..."

They were interrupted by the jingle of the doorbell as some people entered the store, including his mom and Brian. As Mr. Marley turned and walked over to greet them, Andy heard another giggle behind him. He spun around but couldn't see anything amongst the neat rows of baskets. Just as he was convincing himself that he was hearing things, he heard the sound again. This time it was a bit louder and sounded like someone was in the middle of a deep belly laugh. Andy, heart pounding, slowly walked along the rock filled shelves - trying to follow the sound.

"Andy. It's time to go."

His mom's voice, calling from the front of the store, made him jump. Feeling spooked, he hurried towards her -

glancing back several times at the baskets.

"Ready to go?" Brian looked down at him with an affectionate grin.

Andy nodded at Brian and dug his money out of his pocket. When he approached the till to pay for his Thunderegg, Mr. Marley bent down and looked him squarely in the eye.

"Do you understand the task ahead of you?" the store owner asked quietly as he discreetly pointed at Andy's Thunderegg.

Andy was confused at this question, but too shy to ask for an explanation so he just nodded his head and looked at the floor. Mr. Marley put Andy's rock in a black velvet bag and rang in the sale. When he handed the bag to Andy, he winked and whispered, "Good luck".

Back on the highway, Andy made a nest in the back seat amongst pillows and blankets. He had his Thunderegg in his hand and was rubbing it between his thumb and fingers. It was rough, but warmed to his touch. He looked up at the sky and noticed the clouds had changed from a solid grey mass to puffy white marshmallows. Carpets of green trees climbed up the sides of the towering Rocky Mountains. Every once in a while he glimpsed a waterfall tumbling down a rocky path.

Andy, starting to get drowsy, leaned his head against the window. He continued to rub his rock ever so gently and slowly. His eyes started to droop. As he watched the trees and meadows glide past, he wondered what it would be like to ride a horse in the ditch beside the car. In his mind, he saw a white horse galloping so fast it could keep up with the speed of the cars on the highway. It leapt smoothly over anything in its way. He had never ridden a horse before and imagined it would be really exciting. His eyelids sagged and his head felt heavy. Sleepily, he glanced down at his hand as he felt the stone become warmer. It started to tingle and sparkle. Andy squished his eyes closed against the flashes of color that shot out from the dull grey surface.

Chapter 3

WHOOSH! Andy was jostled awake and had a hard time sitting up. The wind was rushing past him so fast he could hardly open his eyes. Feeling something warm and *moving* underneath him, he looked down and squinted against the wind.

"Whoa!!"

He was sitting on a horse! A horse that was galloping very, very fast. Andy fell forward and grabbed the horse around its neck - his heart suddenly hammering against his chest. The Thunderegg was now a pulsing blue and twinkled in his hand. Andy gasped then started to cough from the blast of air that hit his lungs. Digging his heels into the horse's sides for a better grip, he whimpered and buried his face in the long silky mane. Underneath him, the horse surged forward in powerful leaps.

"Uh, 'scuse me. Could you get your heels out of my belly and stop choking me, please," grumbled an irritated throaty voice.

Andy tensed. He glanced over his shoulder to see who was talking to him. There was no one there! It was only him riding this horse that just kept hurtling forward. They leaped over logs and rocks, racing through the long grass. It was actually quite a smooth ride, but Andy was so shocked he couldn't appreciate the thrill of it.

"What?!" whispered Andy in disbelief.

"I said, please stop squeezing me!"

The horse glanced back at Andy and flattened its ears. It was the horse! The horse was talking to him! In his fear, Andy started to let go of the horse's mane and started to slide to one side. He scrambled back to the centre of the horse's back and buried his face in its mane again.

"Please st-st-stop," he whispered.

"Nope. Uh uh. Can't stop till we get there," said the horse.

"G-g-get where? Where are we going? Wh-wh-wh-where are my parents? Who are y-y-y-you?"

"My name is Boo and we're going to wherever your dream ends. Your parents are right beside you in that shiny box." She nodded towards the speeding car beside them. Her breathing was becoming more labored as she continued to surge forward. She answered each question between breaths.

Andy looked to his left and saw the grey ribbon of the highway. Cars rushed by in both directions. Rolling right beside him was his parents' car. His mom sat in the passenger seat - her head bobbing to whatever music she was listening to. Brian's fingers were tapping the steering wheel to the same beat as his mom's jiggles. There was a head leaning against the window in the back seat. It looked like someone had fallen asleep… Wait a minute, thought Andy. That was him! That was *his* head leaning against the window. How could this be? He must be dreaming. He quickly pinched himself as hard as he could.

"Ouch!" he cried.

"No kid, you're not dreaming – I mean this *you* isn't dreaming, *that you* is dreaming." Boo motioned with her nose towards the sleeping figure in the car.

Before Andy could ask another of the hundred questions popping into his head, Boo gasped, "Okay, hang on. Here's a big one."

Horse and rider bounded into the air and flew over a bridge. The cars below disappeared for an instant. Andy's heart skipped a beat as he held his breath. He gripped the horse's mane as hard as he could. When they landed on the ground, on the other side of the bridge, he glanced down at the Thunderegg. It was still a beautiful pulsing blue. He loosened his hold to have a better look just as Boo jumped over a fallen tree. He was caught off guard and the Thunderegg fell out of his hand.

"Oh, n-n-no! My rock!" he cried.

Boo screeched to a halt. Andy thought he was going to fly over her head but managed to stay seated.

"You lost the Dreamstone? Don't tell me you lost the Dreamstone," neighed Boo. She spun around to retrace their path.

"Where did you drop it?" She sounded quite upset. "Here, get off and look."

She gave a little shake and dislodged Andy from her back. He slipped to the ground and landed on his butt. Surrounded by lush green grass, speckled with wildflowers, he sat and stared at Boo. He couldn't make sense of what was going on. Boo continued to stomp circles around him - snorting and swishing her tail.

She was a beautiful white horse with flowing mane and tail. Huge, expressive brown eyes were framed by long, thick lashes. Her elegant, very female nature was in direct contrast to her deep, husky voice.

"Come on, hurry - we're going to lose them."

"L-l-lose who?" Andy mumbled weakly. He was so frazzled, he couldn't think straight.

"We're going to lose your parents and, and .... *you*! Come on, we have to find the Dreamstone." She continued to breathe hard.

Andy correctly assumed it was not from exertion. Boo was very distressed by this turn of events. Her eyes were huge – showing white around the edges. She snorted and stamped her dainty feet. Her ears flipped back and forth and her tail swished from side to side. He figured he'd better do as she said and ask questions later.

Scrambling to his feet, Andy started looking in the grass. The bridge they had leaped over was to their right. Cars continued to stream under it and disappear down the highway. There was a river running beside the highway. Horse and boy slowly made their way towards the river. With heads down, they covered every inch of the grass. Back and forth. Back and forth. They zigzagged until they were at the edge of the river.

Andy - getting over his shock - started to feel braver. He was hot, hungry, thirsty and confused. Without thinking, he stopped in his tracks and stomped his foot.

"Okay, just hold on a m-m-m-minute. What's going on? Wh-wh-where are my parents? How c-c-c-can you talk – you're a h-h-h-horse! Why do we need to f-f-f-find the r-r-r-rock, anyway?"

Boo rolled her huge brown eyes and sighed. Her head drooped and her swishing tail came to a standstill.

"Your parents are driving further and further away in that smelly metal box. With you, I might add. And we'll never find them again if we don't hurry up and find your gemstone." She talked so fast, Andy's head was spinning. "You can't get back into your own body unless you're close enough to see it from this world. And you have to have your Dreamstone with you. And it's a Dreamstone, not a rock. You insult the wizards when you call them rocks. Tch. You should know all this stuff," she grumbled impatiently. "Anyone who's been trusted to carry a Dreamstone knows this. And when you're in Dreamland you can understand our language. Who did you get your Dreamstone from anyway?"

"Dreamstone? W-w-w-wizards? Uh, the r-r-rock store in B-b-b-b-anff. I think the m-m-man's name w-w-w-was Mr. Marley or something. H-h-h-he told me it was a Th-th-th-thunderegg."

Boo jumped backwards, almost falling into the river.

"*Thunderegg*? Oh my. Oh boy…..I've never heard of a Thunderegg coming across with a Dreamer." She looked at Andy with new found respect. "So, what are you supposed to do with it?" she asked softly, eyes huge with curiosity.

Andy tilted his head as he looked at her, "Wh-wh-what? What are you t-t-t-talking about?"

"Anyone that comes across with a Dreamstone has a chance to do something they've always dreamed of. But a Thunderegg is another story. They're rare. And I don't think they're like Dreamstones. I don't quite understand how this is supposed to work." She shook her head as if that would help bring her answers. "Marley the Wizard must have told you what to do with it."

"Mr. M-M-Marley said something about a j-j-journey. But most of the t-t-t-time he talked it sounded like g-g-g-gibberish."

Boo stood there quietly. Her head tilted to one side and her large, unblinking brown eyes glazed over. Andy felt like she was looking right through him. He started to squirm but for some reason couldn't take his eyes away from hers. All of a sudden, it felt like she was inside his head. The memory of his time in the rock store replayed in his mind. It was almost like he was watching a movie. The strange thing was that he wasn't the only one watching it. Boo held his gaze as he remembered the excitement of seeing the shelves and shelves of rocks. The colors, textures and variety of shapes and sizes were overwhelming. He remembered the allure his rock had on him. He watched himself shake his head when his mom tried to convince him to consider a prettier, shinier rock than the one he gripped in his hand. Andy remembered the confusion and awe when he thought he saw his rock twinkle. Mr. Marley, or '*Marley the Wizard*', as Boo called him, came into focus. He remembered the feelings of discomfort as Mr. Marley kept watching him. As the scene played on, it slowed down. He remembered being surprised when he turned from the shelves and discovered that no one else was in the store except for Mr. Marley. The old man started to speak – showing Andy the different gemstones. Then, as he began to explain about the rock in Andy's hand, things slowed down even more. He watched Boo's head jerk up. Her ears twitched back and forth like two fuzzy antennas. She took a step back as she continued to stare into Andy's eyes. The scene finished playing when Andy's parents returned to the store.

As if on cue, Andy was released from the spell and the world around him came back into focus. He could hear the birds chirping in the trees and the water gurgling over the boulders in the river.

It took a few moments for Boo to relax. She quivered and puffed through widened nostrils as she continued to stare at Andy. She cleared her throat and quietly said, "Oh my. You are ....special. Yet, there was some kind of interference with the Wizard's magic. This is not good...."

She was quiet for a few minutes. When she noticed Andy's bewildered look, she sighed and explained how their two worlds were connected.

"Dreamstones are a tool or a key for humans to come into our world. It happens when the human is sleeping and for short periods of time. So, only a part of them comes – in their dreams. When they wake up in your world, they leave this world."

"All Dreamers are supposed to know this stuff before they come....," she mumbled again. Sighing, she continued. "Dreamstones allow people to have adventures that they'd always wanted to have. The adventures are more than just dreams, though. Dreamers really LIVE the dreams."

She went on to explain how people from his world couldn't see what was happening in Dreamland when they were awake. And Dreamers traveling in Dreamworld could see the real world only when they were close to their 'real' bodies. Andy spun around and looked at where the highway used to be. Now, there was only forest and meadows. The car, his parents and his 'real' body were long gone.

Boo was quiet for several heartbeats, and then whispered, "Dreamers must be touching their Dreamstone before they can return to their own world."

It took three more heartbeats for this to sink in. When it did, Andy plopped down in the tall grass and felt very, very tired. He looked over at where Boo was standing, staring off into the distance. Besides her mane and tail gently floating in the breeze, she didn't move a muscle. A magpie came and landed on her glossy back. It waddled around in circles for a minute, then lifted its tail feathers and pooped before flying off. Boo didn't flinch.

Several minutes passed by. Andy's eyelids started to droop. It was getting harder and harder to stay awake. He slowly sunk down onto the grass and pillowed his head on his arm.

Chapter 4

Andy woke several hours later to a gentle warm breath on his cheek. Slowly, he opened his eyes and looked up into two rather large nostrils. He blinked once before letting out a loud shriek. Boo jumped back and snorted - her ears flattened back to show her displeasure.

"Geez kid, you don't have to scream! I was only trying to wake you up slowly." Boo snorted again and waited for him to wake up enough to talk to him.

Andy rolled onto his back and gazed up at the sky. Memories of the events that led him to this strange place came flooding back. Part of him just wanted to go back to sleep so he wouldn't have to deal with it all.

He felt a hard lump under his back, but no amount of squirming found him comfort. With a sigh, he rolled over to see what he was laying on. A faint glow shone through the flattened grass. After carefully moving the long blades aside, Andy gasped and jumped to his feet.

"Hah! Boo! Look!" Andy grabbed the shining gemstone and held it over his head in triumph.

As soon as Boo saw what Andy held in his hand, she started prancing, snorting and spinning in circles. Andy whooped and jumped, waving his hands in the air. He gripped the rock so tight the rough edges bit into his hand. Running to Boo, he threw his arms around her neck.

"Good boy!" She lowered her head and with a weird fling of her neck, swung Andy onto her back. Horse and rider pranced in circles, yahooing and snorting their excitement and relief.

Finally out of breath, Andy slid off Boo's back. Gripping the Thunderegg in both hands, he said, "Okay, B-b-boo, tell me how to get b-b-back. I've got it – I'm t-t-t-touching it. What do I have to do? How d-d-do I get back to m-m-my world?"

Boo stopped prancing and lowered her head. "Uh, well, there's more to this than what I first thought, kid. You see, your Thunderegg is different than a Dreamstone. Normal Dreamstones let you live out a dream here, for a short time. But I don't know how Thundereggs work with dreams. Things have been strange around here lately… there must be something big going on …" her voice drifted off as she glanced around.

"B-b-but, but … what d-d-do I have to do?" demanded Andy.

The horse blinked, bringing Andy back into focus.

"I know Marley the Wizard would never send anyone here unless he was sure they understood and wanted to be here. From what you told me – and what I saw - there were some odd things going on in the wizard's shop. You see, wizards are very powerful and no one dares to play around with their magic. But, someone or something was interfering with Marley's charm."

She looked at him for confirmation, "You said you saw the color green…" When he nodded, she continued.

"And a sound like someone was giggling?"

Again, Andy nodded.

"Well, knowing what pranksters the little people can be … one in particular … I think what happened was a faerie trick. When Mr. Marley was initiating you into this, a faerie was doing some kind of magic that garbled his words so you wouldn't hear it. I just can't figure out how one of us could be in your world....it's just never happened before. Strange…" Boo drifted off in thought again.

Andy brought her back to attention by pulling on her mane.

"What am I s-s-supposed to do?" Andy tried desperately to clamp down on his panic.

"Well, I guess we should go to Faeritonia." Boo squinted into the forest behind her. She took a deep breath and said, "Yup, that's what we need to do. You better put that Thunderegg somewhere safe so we don't have another scare." She shook off the apprehension that had begun to settle around her.

As Andy pulled the black velvet bag out of his pants, he asked, "Fairi – who?"

"Faeritonia. It's the largest Faerie City. Where the Faerie King lives."

"T-t-talking horses, now f-f-faeries. R-r-right," mumbled Andy as he dropped the Thunderegg into the bag then shoved it into the deepest pocket of his pants.

Boo kneeled down - something that Andy had only seen done by a circus horse. She urged Andy to climb onto her back. He hesitated.

Cocking her head to one side, she said, "I guess its time for some riding lessons, huh?"

Andy still didn't budge.

Softly she urged, "Haven't you always wanted to ride a horse?"

He gave her a tiny nod.

"Don't worry. We'll start slowly. You've done really great so far." Boo sounded patient and comforting.

Puffing out his cheeks and slowly blowing out the air, Andy took a tentative step towards the kneeling horse. Gently, he flicked the dried bird dung off of her broad back. He was startled, then burst into a nervous laugh at the horrified squeals of '*eughhhhhh*' and her turned up lip. After climbing aboard, he grabbed onto her thick mane and they started off.

They crossed the river and headed into the forest. Andy glanced back, but there was still no sign of the highway. He was worried about moving farther away from where he last saw his mom and Brian. On the other hand, he was curious about this strange world. He knew he should be terrified about this turn of events but it was a dream, right? His real body would be sleeping. No one would miss him. Might as well enjoy it, he thought as he lifted his chin. And, he was riding a horse!

"Okay. So the trick to riding is to stay in the center of my back. You just have to move with me," Boo explained. "When we go faster, squeeze a LITTLE," she glanced back with a twinkle in her eye, "with your upper leg. Imagine your legs as an upside down V."

Andy wiggled a bit, sitting up straighter.

"Yeah! That's it! So, your upper body is going to move – just a little at a time – with my body. Forwards. Backwards. And side to side. You just need to figure out how to balance with my movements."

They traveled for several hours in the quiet forest - climbing over fallen trees and squishing through soft green moss whenever the trail disappeared.

Finally, Andy's curiosity overcame his shyness and he asked, "How d-d-did you get a n-n-name like 'Boo'?

“My first Dreamer couldn’t say my real name so I’ve been ‘Boo’ ever since.

“What’s your real n-n-name?”

“Booriquzilah.”

“Booa – who?” asked Andy.

“Boo will do,” chuckled the horse.

She told him of different Dreamers she had hosted. “Most of them have always wanted to ride a horse, so I give them the ride of their lives,” she said this with pride. Then, for some reason, she let out a weary sigh and fell into a melancholy silence.

Along the way, they stopped to drink from a bubbling stream. It was surrounded by wildflowers and butterflies. Andy slid off her back and picked strawberries along the bank. They were big and juicy and filled him up quickly. He would have liked to have stayed for awhile, but the break was short lived. Boo was anxious to find the faeries.

Andy often had to lay on his belly as they traveled through the trees, so he wouldn’t be knocked off by overhanging branches. Once in awhile, Andy heard rustling in the underbrush. Boo’s ears would flicker back and forth and Andy could feel her body tense underneath him. But she didn’t say anything, so he relaxed and trusted that she would know if there was danger nearby.

As dusk turned to darkness, Andy drifted into sleep. He lay on his stomach in a semi-spread eagle – an arm and a leg flopping down on each side of her back. She glanced back at him and grinned only as horses can. Boo was growing attached to the little Dreamer. Usually humans only stayed in Dreamland for a few hours before waking up in their own world again.

She was just about to cross a small open meadow when a huge apparition flew overhead.

"Oh!" Boo gasped and swung back around to hide under the trees.

The thumping sound of large wings circling overhead had her shivering in the shadows. When she dared to look up, she saw blood red eyes searching the ground below. An evil power whirled through the air, whispering through the forest.

Boo stood quietly, barely breathing. She was thankful that the Dreamer on her back was asleep or she might have been pressed to explain things that she didn't understand herself.

Eventually, the creature disappeared into the dark sky. Boo didn't move until she was sure it was gone. Even then, she tiptoed around the meadow instead of going out into the open.

The horse trudged through the night - taking the long way around some rocky areas. She didn't want to wake the boy up with sudden or jerky movements.

Not long ago she would have been able to go for days on end - through any terrain - without needing rest or feeling tired. Now, she felt exhausted after only a few hours. She planned on stopping soon - to rest and get directions to the faeries glen from an old friend.

Andy had no idea how far they traveled since he was in a deep dreamless sleep.

Chapter 5

Voices woke him. They were muted and muffled. Occasionally, he heard words such as, '*strange happenings*', '*Thunderegg*', '*wizards*', '*faeries*', and '*chosen one*'. He sat up and looked around. They were at a large pond surrounded by a thick forest. Tall green and brown cattails stood at attention along the perimeter of the water. In the small meadow surrounding the pool, multi-colored wild flowers basked in the sun. The quiet hum of insects droned steadily in the background. There were water lilies the size of dinner plates floating in the pond.

Boo swung her long neck around so she could look at him with her huge brown eyes.

"Sleep well?" she asked softly.

"Yup, thanks," Andy mumbled. "Where are w-w-we?"

"We're at my good friend Ziggy's place. Ziggy, this is Andy. Andy, Ziggy. She nodded toward the ground. Andy squinted but couldn't see anything but green moss.

"Hey dude," rumbled a deep voice.

Andy jerked to attention, almost falling off of Boo's back. His eyes widened and his chin dropped. Whoa, thought Andy. That was the biggest, fattest frog he had ever seen. He missed it at first because it had sunk into and blended with the cushiony moss. It was a mixture of greens and browns, just like any other frog he'd seen. But the most peculiar thing was that it was so *fat*. Its glittering yellow eyes were surrounded by folds of frog flesh. He couldn't see its back legs because of the roll of fat hanging from its belly and resting on the ground. Front legs hung from the sides of his body - looking completely useless. Its mouth was wide and narrow and turned up at the sides in a permanent grin. Andy stared, mouth gaping. He didn't know whether to laugh or be totally grossed out.

Boo cleared her throat, just like Andy's mom did when she was trying to pry some politeness out of him. Finally, he remembered his manners.

"Uh, p-p-p-pleased to meet you Mr..... uh, Z-z-iggy." He gulped and finally managed to pull his eyes away from this hilarious looking creature. "Uh, s-s-sorry," he lamely tried to apologize for staring.

"No problem, man. No worries. I've been packing on the pounds lately. But, what can you do when you're surrounded by an endless buffet?" His tongue snapped out and he caught a fly that fluttered a bit too close. He gulped and ribbetted, then let out a barely audible '*ahhh*'.

Andy could feel Boo shaking underneath him as she tried to contain her laughter. It took all his willpower to not grin as Ziggy caught another fly - going through the same process of gulping and ribbetting his pleasure. Andy was wondering if a frog's ribbett was like a human's burp when Ziggy abruptly stopped feasting and continued the conversation.

"So, Boo's been telling me about you and your ... gemstone. Sounds like you've got an adventure in front of you. Come on down here, son ..." Ziggy was interrupted as another fly buzzed by. His tongue snapped out once again and the gulp and ribbett followed. "Let's have a chat before you two carry on."

Snap, Gulp, Ribbett.

No wonder he was so fat. He never stopped eating! Andy slid off of Boo's back and squatted down beside the frog. Geez! Ziggy stood half way up Andy's lower leg and was just as wide as he was tall. Andy was tempted to reach out and poke him in the belly to see if he was soft or hard.

Snap, Gulp, Ribbett.

Andy glanced up at Boo and saw tears streaming from her eyes as she tried to suppress her laughter. She turned away and started to munch on the grass, snorting to try to hide her giggles.

Snap, Gulp, Ribbett.

"Now, here's the thing kid. You can't go around letting everybody know what you have in your pocket. There've been strange things going on around these parts and you just can't be too careful. I heard some mumblings in the trees that there is something or someone searching for Thundereggs." His voice dropped to a whisper.

Snap, Gulp, Ribbett.

Andy jumped back. That one was right over his head.

"Don't worry – I've got great aim," boasted the frog. "Everyone knows Dreamers carry gemstones, otherwise how would they get here? Know what I mean? So it's no big deal when you walk around with a bulge in your pocket. Let them think it's a run of the mill Dreamstone." Ziggy continued issuing advice while his eyes constantly darted to and fro, looking for his next victim.

Snap, Gulp, Ribbett.

"I haven't heard of a Thunderegg around these parts in a long, long time. Yup, they're pretty rare. Anything that rare is valuable. So, keep that thing close to your chest and be careful who you talk to about it."

Snap, Gulp, Ribbett.

"Now, you gotta get to the little people as soon as you can. It sounds like someone there messed up the spell, so they're gonna have ta fix it. Know what I mean?"

Snap, Gulp, Ribbett.

Boo had wandered off a ways and was doing a lot of snorting and blowing. Her head was turned away so neither frog or boy could see her out of control laughter.

"Faeries are okay. They're honest folk. They'll help ya."

Snap, Gulp, Ribbett.

"Can ya give me a little push over there - into the shade?" Ziggy's eyes motioned to a cool spot beside a stand of willow trees.

Andy raised his eyebrows. Was he serious? Ziggy comically mimicked Andy's eyebrow raising. Andy grinned and crawled on his hands and knees to get closer to Ziggy. He hesitantly reached out and gave the fat frog a gentle push.

"Okay. Do you *see* how big I am? You'll have to put more muscle into it than that!" Ziggy rolled his eyes.

Andy dug his toes and knees into the moss and gave Ziggy a harder push. The frog didn't budge. He put his shoulder into it and pushed harder. Thinking Ziggy would be cold and slimy, Andy was surprised to find him warm, dry and pleasantly squishy with a faint musty smell.

Ziggy started to snicker. Andy got up on his feet, bent down and pushed harder. Ziggy's snickers turned into chuckles. Andy grinned and dug his feet into the soft ground and heaved against the frog. Ziggy's chuckles turned into a snorting belly laugh.

Boo sauntered over and watched as giggling boy shoved against an immovable frog who was gasping for breath between each series of guffaws. She shook her head and rolled her eyes before approaching the duo. Boo shoved her nose under the frog's bulky rear end. Ziggy was unceremoniously lifted into the air and dropped into the shady spot.

Andy could have sworn the ground shook under him. But by that time he was rolling on the ground, holding his stomach as he laughed like he'd never laughed before.

As Ziggy's body settled back into its folds and flab, there was a loud 'p*hhhhtttttt*'. All three stopped laughing for a split second then burst out into even louder guffaws. It never occurred to Andy or Boo that frogs could fart!

The three spent another couple of hours chatting and enjoying each other's company. Boo laid on the ground and rested while Ziggy pointed out some edible flowers and berries for Andy. Finally, it was time to resume their journey.

As Andy and Boo prepared to leave, the frog gasped and exclaimed, "Oh, oh, oh, my FAVOURITE! Ooooooh come here my lovelies…" his voice dropped to an enticing whisper.

Andy and Boo wandered back towards Ziggy's shady spot. They looked at the air where Ziggy was staring with a controlling, hypnotic gaze. There was no sign of the flies that Ziggy had made a steady diet of throughout their visit.

All of a sudden the frog's tongue whipped out of his mouth and, *Snap, snap, snap, Gulp, Riiiiiiiiiiiiiiiiii beeeeeeeeeeeet. "Ahhhhhhhh,"* sighed the frog. "Those mitty mites are the tastiest. And look at them all!" he squealed with glee.

Horse and boy finally saw the cloud of no-see-em fleas hovering above the enormous frog's fat head.

Snap, snap, snap, gulp, Riiiiiiibeeeeeeeeet. This time he actually licked his lips.

Andy and Boo groaned in unison.

"That'll keep him busy for a while," mumbled Boo. "Sheesh, every time I see him he's a roll of fat bigger. I'm getting a little worried about him – he can't even move anymore. I've never heard of a frog popping, but the rate he's going….." She sounded troubled, but sighed and continued, "Come on kid, let's hit the trail. We've got some ground to cover before nightfall."

They traveled through valleys and forests and crossed several rivers. Andy would walk until he became tired and then mount Boo again. He enjoyed her rolling gait as she picked her way along the unseen path that Ziggy had carefully outlined for her.

Moments passed in comfortable silence and then they'd break into conversation again. Andy told Boo about life in his world. Boo had never spent so much time with one Dreamer before and it was nice to finally find out about '*the other side*'. She explained to Andy that only one Dreamer came across at a time. Everyone in her world was aware of Dreamers and accepted their brief appearances as a matter of course. He learned that there was a lot of magic in Dreamland. Andy asked what all the strange happenings were about. Boo said that he would have to ask the Faerie King and then she abruptly changed the subject.

Chapter 6

Dusk fell just as they arrived at a small meadow. A riot of wild flowers covered the field with grass as tall as Andy's waist. He sniffed deeply and closed his eyes in ecstasy. The meadow smelled as sweet as a candy store.

There was a stand of large, leafy trees in the middle of the meadow. It was very quiet. Boo stopped in the shadow of the forest, just outside the perimeter of the field. She waited while Andy slid off her back before telling him that she could go no farther.

"This is Faeritonia. They like horses, but they DO NOT appreciate us on their land. Apparently, years ago, a horse wandered into their meadow. He had a meal of that long, lush grass you see there," Boo licked her lips as she motioned towards the meadow.

"And, well, he left his droppings all over the place."

She rolled her eyes in embarrassment then went on to explain that faeries are a very industrious species, but the removal of the horse dung was a rather disgusting job for such tiny creatures. No one wanted to clean it up. Whenever the King called on anyone to help with the chore, they mysteriously came down with the flu. Or they were just leaving to visit their relatives in the neighboring faerie city – any excuse not to be stuck with the smelly job. The meadow stunk for days. Some faeries actually moved into the forest until the Faerie King could figure out a solution to the stinky problem.

"Sit under that tree over there, by the edge. I'll stay here. If you need me, just call."

"B-b-but how do they know I'm h-h-here?" Andy started to panic. "What d-d-do I do? Wh-wh-what do I say?"

Boo was the only familiar thing in this strange place, even if she was a talking horse. He didn't want to be alone. Gently, Boo nudged Andy towards the meadow.

"You'll be fine. You'll know exactly what to say and do when the time comes. Just find the King. Tell him what you told me. He'll help you."

With a groan, Andy trudged to the designated tree and slid down the trunk to rest on the spongy ground. He cradled his now sparkling green Thunderegg in his palm and wondered what was going to happen next.

His thoughts turned to his mom. He wondered what her reaction would be when she couldn't wake the 'real' him up. They must have taken his body to a hospital by now. It saddened him to think of her being so worried and frantic about him. On the other hand, he was starting to enjoy being a '*Dreamer*'. He'd always wanted to ride a horse and his memories of Ziggy made him chuckle. And he was looking forward to meeting the '*little folk*' as Boo fondly called them. Neither Boo or Ziggy seemed to notice his stuttering. He sighed and hoped that no one else in this world would either.

As darkness fell, the peaceful quiet was replaced by a gentle rustling in the distance. Andy could see tiny floating lights appear amongst the stand of trees. As minutes passed, the moving, twinkling lights became more numerous. They slid down the trunks of the trees and meandered through the tall grass. They landed on grass blades and flowers or continued to float through the trees. There were some clusters of lights in spots and many other single ones hovering or gliding through the air. He sat there mesmerized - watching the tiny world of moving lights.

A faint whirring sound, accompanied by tiny voices and laughter grew louder as a group of three tiny lights headed straight towards Andy. He scrambled to his feet, ready to run. Hearing Boo's reassuring snort behind him, Andy relaxed, knowing that she would be there if he needed her.

As the lights drifted closer, they slowed down. The giggling and chatter subsided. Andy could finally see the outline of the three creatures that approached him. The closer they came, the farther he tilted his head in awe.

All three faeries were dressed in green. Their wings fluttered as quickly as a hummingbird's. And the light emitting from each of them came from their chest and shone through their clothing. They all had long green eyes and pointy eyebrows. But that's where the similarities stopped. When you looked closely enough, the faeries were quite obviously different from each other. The largest was no longer than his palm. A very angular face framed a pointy chin and upturned nose. He had spiky hair and long limbs and unusually large feet. Narrow, wide lips turned up in a crooked grin.

Another of the faeries was on the heavy side and Andy was sure he was looking a bit flushed and out of breath. He had a jolly face and his head was covered with curly blond hair. The tiny buttons on his jacket strained and threatened to pop at any minute.

The third faerie was a tiny girl. She was holding hands with the tubby faerie. She half hid behind his vigorously pumping wings. Her hair was blond as well, but straight and hanging in two side pony tails. Innocent and curious eyes were huge in her tiny face. Her head was cocked to one side as she stared up at Andy.

The three faeries hovered in the air about two feet away from Andy's face. Very gradually, 'Tubby', as Andy had silently nicknamed him, started to drop. His face was turning red and tiny beads of sweat were popping out on his forehead.

Andy cleared his throat and because he was nervous, said rather loudly, "Uh, w-w-would you like m-m-me to sit d-d-down?"

All three faeries tumbled backwards. The tall gangly faerie righted himself quickly. Then he helped Tubby and the little girl stop rolling and falling through the air. After they had pulled themselves together, they tentatively re-approached Andy.

As they got nearer, the gangly faerie said, in a tiny annoyed voice, "That would be appreciated, thank you. And by the way, we can hear you just fine if you whisper. We're not deaf, you know. "

"Right. Sorry," mumbled Andy as he slowly sat down.

The creatures floated to the ground in front of his crossed legs. As soon as Tubby's feet hit the ground, he plunked down on his round bottom and heaved a sigh of relief. His wings drooped behind him. The smallest faerie climbed into his lap and stuck her thumb in her mouth - her huge eyes never leaving Andy's face.

The taller faerie stepped forward to make the introductions.

"My name's Tobee. This is Barry and that's his little sister, Gertie." Andy had to listen very closely as Tobee's voice was quite small.

"Um, hi. I'm A-A-Andy," he spoke quietly so as not to send the faeries tumbling into the tall grass surrounding them. Not sure how to explain the very strange situation he found himself in, he hesitated. He knew he had to speak with the King and didn't think they would let him until he gave some sort of explanation. So he took a deep breath and started his story.

"Uh, I'm s-s-s-supposed to talk to the K-k-k-king who Ziggy said could help me get back home. B-b-b-boo – she's a h-h-h-horse – brought ......me ......here......," his voice dwindled off as Gertie jumped out of Barry's lap and started flitting towards the forest.

"Boo? Boo's here? Where is she? Boo! Boo..... BOO.....BOOOOOOOOOOOO!"

As Gertie's little voice bellowed as loud as she could (which was still a very tiny sound to Andy), she zoomed off into the dark forest in the direction where Boo was grazing.

Barry hauled himself to his feet and took off in lumbering pursuit.

"Gertie! Get back here. You know you're not supposed to go into the forest alone. Wait for me." Their voices receded into the darkness. Finally, Andy heard Boo's soft welcoming nicker.

"We won't see them again tonight – Boo and Gertie have a special bond after Boo saved her..." Tobee's voice drifted off as he remembered the scary incident a few months back. He shivered, grimaced and brought his attention back to the giant sitting in front of him.

"Okay, so I get the drift. Somehow you got stuck in Dreamland. Now you need some help getting back?"

Andy dragged his eyes away from the forest where he could still hear Boo's happy snorting, and focused on Tobee.

"W-w-w-well, yeah," said Andy. He was relieved he wouldn't have to explain the whole story.

"No problem," smiled Tobee. "First thing we're gonna have to do is get you down to a decent size so you don't squash anyone. Hold on - I haven't done this in a while."

Tobee started chanting some sort of strange incantation. The light in his chest became brighter. As Andy's toes started to tingle, he shoved his Thunderegg into his hoodie's front pocket. As the tingling turned to ticklishness, it moved from his toes to his knees, upper body and arms. He tried not to giggle, but being ticklish by nature, he couldn't help it and burst out laughing. His vision blurred for a heart beat and then, BAM! He was sprawled on the ground, still giggling and feeling quite out of breath.

When his vision cleared he found himself staring into a pair of laughing green eyes.

"That's better! Now you're not so big and ugly."

Andy blinked and realized that Tobee was the same size as he was. Or rather *he* was the same size as Tobee! He scrambled to his feet and looked around. Everything looked huge. Blades of grass, now an arms' length wide, towered over him. It was like being in the forest again, only the trees were giant blades of grass.

All of a sudden Andy heard a loud rustling sound from directly behind him. He spun around, eyes huge with fright. Out from behind the wall of grass sauntered a huge creature. It was as tall as he was and just as wide with a hard thorny shell. It had at least six legs and long, searching antennas. The menacing red eyes were huge and stared right at Andy. Gasping, he stumbled backwards. If Andy was his normal size, this beast would have been as big as his foot. The hairs on the back of his neck stood straight up and his heart hammered in his chest. He lost his balance and started to fall. The angry creature scuttled towards him.

"WHOA!" All of a sudden he was airborne. Tobee had grabbed him by the arm and shot up into the air.

"Whew! Close one!" Tobee chuckled nervously as they flitted between and around flower stalks and grass blades.

"He must have been within the circle of magic. Geez! No matter how hard I practice these days, every time I do a charm something gets messed up." He continued grumbling to himself as they rose above the forest of grass.

Andy, heart pounding, mouth hanging open, couldn't believe what was happening. Here he was, flying through the air with a faerie gripping his arm. He panicked and grabbed Tobee around the waist.

"You aren't g-g-going to d-d-d-drop me, are you? Aren't I too h-h-h-heavy for you?"

"Aw, heck no," Tobee exclaimed. "We faeries are strong for our size. Plus, I added a lightweight spell to the shrinking charm. You're as light as a feather."

"B-b-but, I'm afraid of heights! I'm g-g-gonna be sick!" Andy waited for his stomach to start rolling.

Tobee looked at him, one eyebrow raised. "Hmmm. Well, would you rather walk through the grass with our new friend, or trust me to do what faeries do best?"

Andy glanced back to where the creepy critter was still rustling in the grass and shuddered.

"Awww, man," he mumbled. He started counting under his breath, just like his mom had told him to do on the Gondola Ride.

When Tobee heard his quiet counting, he grinned and sped up.

Andy tried to relax as they made their way toward the trees in the middle of the meadow. As the night sky became darker, the faerie lights became brighter and more numerous.

"We'll go hang out at my place for the night. You won't be able to see the King until tomorrow anyway," stated Tobee.

Andy didn't reply. He was so absorbed in the sights and

sounds they passed as they meandered their way towards the grove, that he didn't notice he'd stopped counting.

There were faeries gently pulling leaves and petals from sleeping flowers and carting them back towards the trees. Others were, with great effort, tearing blades of grass lengthwise, making long green ropes. These too, were dragged back towards the stand of trees.

Suddenly, Tobee dropped to the ground pulling Andy along with him. In the distance were the sounds of terrified screams coming from other faeries. Their chest lights disappeared as they, too, hid in the grass or flew into the trees for cover. A heavy beating sound emerged from the dark sky above. Andy had landed under Tobee's trembling body. He managed to peek out from under the faerie's arm and look up into the night sky. A huge shadow slowly passed over the meadow. A pair of menacing red eyes scanned the now dark and quiet field. Within moments it was gone.

Tobee, breathing a sigh of relief, grew limp, his full weight on top of Andy.

"Scuse m-m-me," Andy puffed and pushed against Tobee, trying to roll him off.

"Oh, sorry!" Tobee rolled over and lay sprawled on the ground beside Andy. "That was close," he mumbled under his breath.

"What was th-th-that?" demanded Andy.

"Uhhhh. Well, we're not sure. But it's not good."

"Huh?"

"Okay, you know what? You're gonna have to talk to the King, 'cause I'm gonna get in trouble if I say anything. So, let's go."

Tobee jumped to his feet, grabbed Andy by the arm and zipped up into the sky. Other lights hesitantly appeared and the meadow quietly buzzed with the sounds of subdued voices. Several times, Andy tried to talk to Tobee about the shadow, but the faerie refused to discuss it.

When they finally reached the tree trunks, they flapped their way straight up until they reached the leafy umbrella. Hundreds of faeries were whizzing up and down on a myriad of errands. Lights could be seen at every little corner or indent in the large branches and trunks of the tree. Faeries were everywhere. Some were lounging in their holes while others moved from branch to branch, busying themselves with different chores or activities. A few were struggling upwards with leaves shaped like buckets - the stems twisted into handles. The buckets were full of water. Andy was sure that one drop, maybe two, was all that was needed to fill their pails. Other faeries were sweeping out their holes with a shredded piece of yellowed grass. Tiny faeries – smaller than Gertie - played hide and seek in the leaves. A small chattering crowd of children followed them until Tobee shooed them away. Through all the activity and chatter, Andy could sense an underlying tension. The adult faeries were somber. They glanced at Tobee and Andy as they flew by, but made no attempt to greet them. They looked tired and distracted.

"How m-m-m-many faeries live here?"

"I think the last count was about 239 families. The King lives at the crown of the tree and everybody else has a place of their own. We're the biggest faerie city around," he boasted. After a minute of silence, he added quietly, "Although we haven't had any babies born in awhile. Don't know what that's all about."

They fluttered under a huge leaf and landed on a branch.

"Here's my place," Tobee announced proudly. "Older faeries or faerie families get to live closer to the trunk. I just moved out, so I have to start out here."

He waited until Andy got his balance before letting go of his sleeve and leading the way inside his home. It was a snug little hole. A small kitchen boasted hand-me-down dishes and pots. Swinging in one corner was a hammock bed made of woven grass blades. Mushrooms carved into the shape of a table and two chairs sat in the centre of the room.

While Andy settled himself on a mushroom stool, Tobee brought out dishes and cups and bowls of food. Andy was famished and didn't ask what he was eating. It tasted delicious and his appetite was soon sated.

Tobee was very curious about humans and life in Andy's world. It didn't take long for Andy to relax as he felt more comfortable with the faerie. The conversation was easy as Tobee took no notice of Andy's stutter and encouraged him to talk. Andy told him all about his life in Saskatoon, what he did at school, and his favorite sport - baseball.

"I can't believe you don't have any brothers or sisters," Tobee said. "I've got seven kids in my family. And that's small compared to the rest of the faeries!"

Andy explained that his dad died years ago and that his mom had just remarried. He found himself talking about Brian and how he just couldn't call him '*dad*'.

The only magic that Andy had seen was card tricks and pulling bunnies out of hats. Tobee raised his eyebrows at this since magic was so common place in his world. Faeries learned and used what spells they needed in everyday life.

But Tobee didn't tell Andy how the Master Magician was so weak and sickly he could hardly cast a simple spell anymore. Or how other faeries who were expert with certain charms had lately had a hard time getting them right, no matter how hard they tried. It was a little worrisome when a simple spell to carry a bucket of water up the tree turned into a huge downpour. As a result, less and less faeries were using magic. This made the usually happy and playful adults into tired grumps.

Andy couldn't remember ever talking so much. His stuttering didn't seem to bother Tobee at all. Andy was relaxed and felt at ease with the faerie. He knew that he could trust him.

He told Tobee about the Banff Rock & Gem Store, Marley the Wizard, falling asleep in his parent's car and waking up on Boo's back. As he was telling Tobee how kind both Boo and Ziggy had been to him, he choked up a little and realized how alone and lost he would have been without their help.

All of a sudden, his right leg started to tingle. His Thunderegg! He pulled it out of his pocket and held it up. Tobee gasped and jumped to his feet, knocking his stool over in the process.

"Oooooooooooh! You didn't tell me it was a Thunderegg," whispered Tobee. He couldn't take his eyes off of the rock that was slowly pulsing a reddish purple color.

"What is a Th-th-th-thunderegg, anyway?" asked Andy. "And why d-d-d-do they change colors all the t-t-time?"

"Thundereggs have special powers. Wizards guard them and are pretty secretive about them. That's about all I know....wow!" He gazed reverently at the gemstone.

"So, w-w-w-what am I supposed to do with it?" asked Andy.

"If Marley the Wizard gave it to you, he must have told you what to do with it. What did he tell you?" Tobee looked confused.

"When he s-s-s-started talking about it, his w-w-w-words were all jumbled and made no sense. When ...," Andy was interrupted by Tobee.

"His words sounded jumbled? Did you see or hear

anything else when this was happening?" Tobee's sudden urgency startled Andy.

"Well, I saw f-f-f-flashes of green out of the corner of my eye, but I c-c-c-couldn't see what it was."

"Flashes of green?" Tobee's face paled, his hands gripped the edge of the table.

Andy, head tilted, stared at Tobee. "Uh, yeah.... And th-th-there was a giggling s-s-sound..."

"Hawh! That's her. Oh, wow! She made it through." Tobee leaped into the air, fists raised in triumph. After performing a butt jiggling dance, an assortment of yee haws and yips to accompany the show, Tobee finally plopped back into his chair.

Andy didn't know whether he should be concerned for his new friend's mental health or be excited with him.

"It's my cousin - Lucy. She made it. Everyone thought she was gone for good. Dead. Never to be seen again. Hah! I knew she could do it."

If Tobee's grin got any bigger, Andy was sure his face would split. He squinted at the faerie, trying to make sense of what he was talking about.

Tobee snickered at Andy's look and took a breath before explaining. "Lucy and I have been trying to get into your world for years. Everyone else around here is so boring. They never want to leave our home meadow let alone our world. But, we want *adventure*. We want to see the world. Our world *and* yours." Tobee's green eyes brightened with excitement.

"We've gotten into a few predicaments." his eyes dropped in embarrassment. "But we usually find our way out on our own," he added, defensively. "Lucy's been gone for almost a month now. I've been looking for her as much as I can, but I've already gotten into trouble with the King. See, we're never allowed to use that kind of magic. I don't know how she did it. And Marley the Wizard must not have known she was there. If he found her or knew that she went across, sparks would be flying! No one ever dares interfere with Wizard magic."

They chatted for a while longer before both started to yawn. It was getting lighter outside and time for all faeries to sleep. Andy didn't have any problem with that idea - he was exhausted. Tobee quickly made up another bed. It was soft green moss packed into a leaf that hung from the roof. Andy was asleep before the hammock-bed stopped swinging.

Chapter 7

Tobee shook Andy awake when the moon showed its face in the night sky. It took Andy a few minutes to figure out where he was and who the pointy nosed fellow with the lopsided grin was. Memories flooded his sleep fogged brain. Had it been three days already? His mom must be so worried about him. He was enjoying this little adventure, but he knew he'd be in a lot of trouble if he didn't get back to … get back to where? He didn't even know where his parents were! Tobee shoved a piece of bread (it's probably the size of a crumb in my world, thought Andy) and a cup of cocoa into his hands, interrupting his thoughts.

"Come on, we gotta go meet the King. I left a message with his steward while you were sleeping and told him everything. I'm sure he's figured out something by now," said Tobee brightly.

They quickly gobbled their breakfast and started their downward flight towards the King's attendance area.

King Ferbinsol was old, with a white beard and neatly combed hair under his crown. He looked weary even though it was early evening and just the beginning of his day.

"My ma says there are rumors that King Ferbinsol is sick or something. He's ruled, like, forever, and never gets sick. But in the last few months, his hair's turned grey, he's bent over and always looks tired. He can barely fly by himself anymore!" whispered Tobee just before he was ushered forward to meet with the King.

Andy, left standing under a leaf, gazed at the King with curiosity then strained his ears to hear what he said to Tobee.

"I'm glad to hear your mother is well, Tobee. Please give her my regards."

Through with niceties, King Ferbinsol got right down to business.

"So, it seems you believe young Lucy made it through to the human world."

"Yes sir. I do. You see…" Tobee's excited outburst was interrupted by the King's bellow.

"ENOUGH! I'll hear no more of this nonsense. You know it's not possible."

"Yes sir," mumbled Tobee. He stared at the ground and gently kicked at an imaginary something by his foot.

The King slumped in his throne, looking deeply troubled and unhappy. He sat there for several moments, deep in thought, until an attendant, standing behind the throne, gently cleared his throat.

Sighing, the King straightened up and commanded, "Bring the young Dreamer forward."

Andy stepped tentatively towards the throne. The King apologized for the magical mess that he was presently in and asked to see his 'gemstone'. Andy dug into his pocket and brought out his Thunderegg. There were some quiet gasps from the stewards standing behind the King. King Ferbinsol blinked once, and then sat back in his throne.

"So, it *is* a Thunderegg," he muttered. "Hmmph…" he drifted off into thought.

Again, the steward cleared his throat - bringing the

King's attention back to the nervous Dreamer and faerie standing in front of him. King Ferbinsol knew what had to be done but was concerned about sending the boy off by himself. He motioned for Tobee to step forward. A long quiet conversation ensued between the two. Andy watched as Tobee stood up straighter and firmly nodded his head in agreement to something the King said. The King asked another question and Tobee nodded again. When King Ferbinsol waved his hand, Tobee kneeled at the foot of the throne. The King put a hand on the young faerie's shoulder and quietly said a few more words. Tobee stepped back from the throne, bowed and returned to where Andy was waiting. He had a proud and determined look on his face. Andy couldn't help but wonder what the exchange was all about.

The King sat up straighter and motioned Andy forward. He took a deep breath and hesitantly stepped forward.

"I'm going to get right to the point here, son. We don't have any time to waste," began the King. "You probably already know about how Dreamstones work between your world and ours, so I won't get into that. Thundereggs are a different story. They are *not* meant to be used as a Dreamer's gemstone. Now, you, coming across with one, leads me to believe that something is terribly wrong. There've been too many unexplainable events and they're becoming more common every day," he drifted off into thought. A steward cleared his throat.

The King continued, with an apologetic look. "It's my belief that through some wizardly kind of magic, you have been sent here with the Thunderegg for a reason. I know this must all be a bit overwhelming for you….." the King hesitated before continuing. "Thundereggs are the base of our magic. They are scattered all over the land. Something has been happening to them. And for one to show up with a Dreamer is just too much for me to figure out." He sighed and shook his head. "Well, there's nothing else to be done about it. I'm afraid your journey won't be over until your Thunderegg is delivered to the Gemstone Wizard. If anyone knows what this is all about, it will be him."

The King chuckled at Andy's confused and worried look.

"Don't worry, son. You wouldn't have been chosen by Marley the Wizard if you weren't up to the task. Tobee has agreed to show you and Boo the way there."

Andy was about to ask one of many questions, when the King continued.

"You two should be on your way. No time to waste." His gaze shifted from Andy to Tobee and back to Andy again. It was obvious that he was finished with the issue and was dismissing them.

As they turned to go, the King stopped them. Looking into Andy's eyes, he gravely said, "Keep your gemstone hidden. At all costs. You may not know who is friend or foe until it's too late."

Andy's stomach tightened in apprehension. He quickly stuffed the Thunderegg back into its bag and then safely into his pocket before turning to leave.

"Safe journey," the King murmured - brow creased in worry - as he watched them leave.

Chapter 8

Tobee and Andy packed a small bag of food.

"I just have to make a quick stop before we go," Tobee said as they left his hole.

They headed towards the trunk, along the same branch that Tobee's home was on. As they got closer to the trunk, Andy could hear a loud racket coming from a hole hidden behind a leafy branch. There was a woman's nattering voice and the sound of several children playing. When they ducked through the doorway, the children's chattering turned to squeals. Tobee was bombarded with faeries of all different sizes. They hugged him and pulled on his wings to get his attention.

"Hey mom," Tobee called to the short, squat lady faerie. She was working away in the kitchen and glanced up at his voice. Her continuous conversation moved from her younger children to her oldest without missing a beat.

"Tobee! My first born. How is it with you?" She rushed over to envelop Tobee in a crushing hug. "And who do we have here?" She squinted up at Andy.

Tobee made the introductions, and then quickly explained that the King had given orders for him to escort Andy to the Gemstone Wizard. Tobee's mother did not like the idea one bit. But she couldn't argue with the King. His decisions were always final. Anyone daring to cross him was banished from the city. He was a good and fair King - lenient with young faeries' antics while they were growing up, he had no patience for adults who didn't follow his rules or decisions.

"Well, you take care of yourself. Remember your manners. Don't get lost and...." The instructions continued nonstop for several minutes. Tobee knew better than to interrupt her, so he just nodded and continued to say, "Yes, ma'am. No, ma'am."

She was finally distracted when one of Tobee's younger siblings spilled the jam she had been making. As she rushed over to scold the child and clean the mess, Tobee and Andy made a hasty retreat.

They left the meadow and found Boo waiting restlessly in the forest. She had a nomadic spirit and was used to being on the move. Spending any more than a day and a half in one spot made her antsy. Her welcoming neigh made Andy smile and he urged Tobee to fly faster. When they finally were close enough to greet each other, Tobee placed Andy on the ground, stood back and performed a quick growth charm. Andy zoomed to his normal size and promptly plopped onto the ground.

"Whoa!" he exclaimed. "M-m-maybe a little s-s-slower next t-t-time, Tobee?"

Andy had to strain to hear Tobee's tiny chuckle. He bent down, scooped the faerie up in his hand and plopped him onto his shoulder. Tobee's 'whoop' and flutter of wings was followed by a fit of giggles by both boys.

After catching their breaths, they turned back to Boo. Her head was cocked to one side, one ear flopped back, the other one trained on them. Her huge eyes blinked once and she sighed.

"Are you two finished?"

The boys grinned sheepishly. Tobee quickly explained to Boo what the King's instructions were. She was to take them to a distant mountain range to find Kailani, a bald eagle that would guide them through the next leg of their journey. Tobee had memorized the King's directions and repeated them to Boo. She nodded and then kneeled down so Andy could mount.

They circled the faeries' glen and headed off in a north-westerly direction. Within minutes Tobee was brushed off of Andy's shoulder by an overhanging branch. He did some interesting aerial acrobat moves before finally finding his wings and righting himself in midair. He looked a bit queasy, so Andy stuck out his hand for the faerie to sit and regain his balance.

"Hmmmm," mumbled Boo, "Do ya think maybe he could ride in one of your pockets?"

Boo had visions of having to stop every few minutes to first of all find the faerie in the dark then wait until he got his breath back. She'd had a good rest, but knew the journey to the mountain where Kailani lived was a long and difficult trek. Her speed and energy were diminishing daily. She needed to rest more often and for longer periods of time. Not only was she concerned about carrying out her part in this mission, she had sensed some urgency in the King's message.

Andy pulled the hood of his sweater out behind him and held it open for Tobee to scamper into. The faerie rearranged himself so his upper body hung over the edge of the hood just behind Andy's ear. He had a great view, could still talk with Andy and Boo and was safe from swinging branches.

They continued on their way at a much faster pace. Boo and Tobee would occasionally discuss a questionable turn or directional change. But most conversation revolved around questions from Boo and Tobee about Andy's '*real*' life. The night wore on as the travelers kept a steady pace. At regular intervals Andy would jump off and walk for a while, claiming that he needed to stretch his legs. The truth was that he was concerned about Boo becoming over tired and not able to lead the way. But lead the way she did. Andy followed in her footsteps, hanging on to her long, silky tail as she picked her way through the dark, quiet forest.

Eventually, Andy asked "So Boo, how d-d-do you know G-G-Gertie so well?"

"Oh, we ran into each other – literally - a while back. Cute kid."

"Uh huh……and…?" pressed Andy when she didn't continue.

"Well, she was lost. So I took her back home."

Andy waited expectantly to hear more details.

"Tch," clicked Tobee. "Boo, why don't I tell Andy the story?"

"You might as well. No use trying to keep it a secret," she grumbled.

"Boo is a hero in Faeritonia. She saved Gertie's life….well, Boo, its true!" Tobee looked her in the eye as she stopped and swung her head around, ears pinned back.

"Oh, whatever." Boo shook her head in embarrassment and continued down the trail.

Tobee whispered in Andy's ear, "It's true. She just doesn't like all the attention." Out loud, he continued, "A couple of months ago, Gertie and Barry's family were going to visit relatives in Fairstoke. That's the faerie village on the other side of the forest." He arranged himself more comfortably on Andy's shoulder before continuing.

"It's a long night's flight. Especially when you have to fly at a kid's speed," he added. "They got to the lunch spot –

it's about half way there - and stopped to eat and let the little ones rest. Gertie saw some fireflies and went to play hide and seek with them. When the family was ready to go again, they couldn't find Gertie. So they started searching."

Boo cut in here, "Yeah, in the wrong direction."

"I know, Boo. But they have thirteen kids. And four of them are younger than Gertie. It's hard to keep track of everyone," Tobee tried to defend the faeries.

"So why do you faeries have so many kids? Huh? We horses have one at a time. We wait until they can take care of themselves, then we have another one."

"I don't know," Tobee said. "It's just the faerie way, I guess. My dad always says, '*The more beams to light the night, the happier we'll be.*'"

"Humph," grunted Boo.

"Anyway, Boo was traveling through the same forest...."

"I was on an errand for the Mermaid Queen," corrected Boo with a sniff.

"Right," Tobee rolled his eyes. "Well, she heard a commotion by a Magic Spot. So, she snuck as close as she could get..."

"Wh-wh-what's a Magic Spot?"

"They're sacred places. Scattered all over the land. Anyway, Boo snuck as close as she could get..."

"I did not sneak. I went quietly and under cover. If you hadn't noticed my coat, it's white. I have to stay in the shadows if I don't want to be seen. Plus, it was close to a Magic Spot. We should start calling them Danger Spots," she ended off in a mumble.

"As she got closer," Tobee ignored Boo's indignant

interruption, "she saw a faerie light coming towards her at full speed. Before she knew it, Gertie crashed into her and knocked her over."

"Oh, right! A little flea of a thing is going to knock *me* over!" Boo stopped in her tracks, swung her head around, ears back, and glared at Tobee.

Tobee snickered into his hands.

When Boo realized that he had egged her on, she rolled her eyes and said, "Okay, you goof. I'll tell the rest of the story. Geez." She continued along the trail and gathered her thoughts.

"Gertie crashed into me alright. She almost knocked herself out. Poor little thing was so scared. It took a few minutes before I could finally understand what she was saying. She kept repeating, '*Fire*' and '*monster*' and '*red eyes*'."

"You m-m-mean like the thing that f-f-flew over last night?" Andy interrupted.

"Yup. I wanted to go and investigate. I heard thumping and scraping and snorting sounds coming from the Magic Spot."

"Everybody knows that you're not supposed to disturb Magic Spots," piped in Tobee.

"But Gertie was so scared, I couldn't take her with me and I didn't want to leave her alone."

Andy could tell by Boo's worried voice that she was reliving the scene.

"So, she hid under my mane and we turned around and headed back toward Faeritonia. It was almost dawn when we finally ran into one of the search parties. I ended up taking the whole family back to Faeritonia. They were all too exhausted and upset to continue their holiday."

“Gertie hasn’t stopped talking about ‘her Boo’ since then,” added Tobee. “It seems like you have quite the singing voice, Boo….,” hinted Tobee.

“Nope. Uh uh. Forget it. I only sing in emergency situations or in private,” she answered stubbornly.

“Tch, chicken,” muttered Tobee under his breath.

“So, wh-wh-what about the M-m-magic Spot?” pressed Andy.

“Well, I went back the next day and the whole Meadow was dug up. It looked like someone had lit fires all over it. Trees were uprooted - it was a mess,” the concern in Boo’s voice was noticeable.

“The worst part,” added Tobee, “is that she said the power was gone from the area.”

“P-p-power?”

“Yeah - magic power. When you’re near a Magic Spot, the air just thrums with power,” explained Tobee.

“It’s just like all the rumors we’ve been hearing. Only this was too close to home,” Boo mumbled.

“So, it was just…..g-g-gone?” puzzled Andy.

“Yeah”

“Yup”

“Huh”

“And the red eyed night shadow is showing up more often,” Tobee quietly added as all three gazed up at the black sky.

At dawn, they arrived at a large lake with a sandy beach. Boo tried to hide her weariness but both Andy and Tobee could tell by her drooping head and tail, that she needed a rest. With an unspoken agreement, the boys scampered off towards the beach to play in the water.

Boo gratefully dropped to her side, nose balanced on the ground and fell into an exhausted sleep.

Tobee got the knack of fluttering along beside Andy's ear so Andy could hear what he was saying.

Andy removed his runners, rolled up his pants and splashed in the water along the shore. The sand was a fine, white, powdery grain. It was soft on the feet and great for building sandcastles. Over the next few hours, they built a small medieval city. The castle was in the centre - its many turrets were tall and finger thin. They created pointy roofs on each tower. Small twigs acted as flag poles. The castle walls were high and thick and covered with many tiny windows and doorways. The surrounding moat divided the castle from the city. In comparison to the detailed castle, the houses were simple, square boxes.

Andy made up daring stories of knights in battle. When he started to create a dragon out of soggy leaves and small branches, Tobee became quiet. Andy's dragon became an evil, fire breathing demon. The knights of Andy's imagination had difficulty protecting the castle from the monster's onslaughts. Tobee sat on top of a small branch that acted as the bridge over the moat. He listened to Andy's story with growing concern.

By noon, they were both yawning. A shady spot under a large tree with overhanging boughs was chosen as the best place to curl up. Within minutes both boys had dozed off.

Hours later, they were startled awake by a warm breath of air on their faces. It was a good thing that Tobee had rolled himself into a ball in the curve of Andy's neck. If he hadn't he would have been blown into the tree trunk and injured a wing. Boo snickered at their startled faces and stepped back. She continued to breakfast in a small grassy area and gave them some time to wake up.

The boys grumbled, stretched and pulled their bodies into sitting positions. Nothing was said before, during or after Tobee's mumbled shrinking chant to get Andy down to size for breakfast. The only way that the crumbs in Tobee's backpack would fill Andy's stomach would be if Andy was Tobee's size while he ate.

Besides passing bread back and forth between them, neither one moved. Once breakfast was complete, Tobee mumbled the growing charm and Andy was his normal size once again. He stooped over, scooped up the faerie and placed him on his shoulder. Yawning, they made their way to where Boo was waiting and the three set off.

Within an hour, Boo was rolling her eyes at the boys' goofiness. They had fun together – making up stories and telling jokes. They walked as much as they could - scampering ahead of Boo to play hide and seek. Tobee was usually the winner as it was so easy for him to hide. The faerie would often tell tales of tricks that one faerie had played on another. Tears of laughter streamed down Andy's cheeks as he pictured the scenes in his mind. He found out that Lucy and Tobee were the worst tricksters. Or rather *best* tricksters if you thought about the creativity it took to come up with some of the ideas they had. Now that Lucy was gone, things were much quieter around Faeritonia. Tobee sighed and his wings drooped when he thought about how his world was changing.

At dusk, they took a short break in a sparsely wooded area by a small, muddy creek. The boys realized they were starving. So once again, Tobee rattled off his shrinking charm. He had a glint in his eye as he did it. But before Andy could say anything, he was rocketing back down to the ground.

"Tobee, you're g-g-gonna regret th-th-that," Andy rubbed his bruised behind as he hauled himself to his feet. He jumped on the faerie, wrapping his arms around his gangly green legs. Tobee leaped into the air, dragging Andy with him. He hovered in the air while Andy screamed and kicked his legs. Slowly Tobee floated over to a mossy patch and unceremoniously dropped him onto the cushiony patch. By that time, Andy was laughing so hard, he had no energy to wallop Tobee when the faerie finally floated within reach - a huge grin on his face.

After their break, Andy was restored to his own size and they prepared to leave. Just as he was about to mount Boo, her body tensed, ears perked forward. With neck arched, she sniffed quietly out of her large nostrils.

"What's wrong," Andy whispered when she didn't move or say anything.

"Shhh," she shushed him then nosed him into the bush. "Crawl under there and DON'T MOVE."

She trotted to the creek and rolled in the mud until every inch of her was covered. Only the whites of her frightened eyes showed as she hurried back to the bushes. She looked like a shadow. Andy's mouth hung open during this whole scene. If he'd learned anything about his horse friend it was that she hated being dirty.

It wasn't long before his human ears picked up what her horse ears had heard moments earlier. There was a thumping sound in the night air. And it was fast approaching their hiding place.

"Should I shrink him?" the quivering Tobee whispered to Boo.

"No! We don't know if it can detect magic. Just be still."

Andy watched as a large apparition crossed the starless sky. It passed in front of the moon. Andy gasped as he thought he recognized the shape of a dragon from one of his old fairytale books. It was gone as quickly as it appeared. Boo's sigh of relief woke the boys from their terrified trance.

"Is.... it.......g-g-gone?" Andy whispered.

All three stared at the quiet, still sky.

"Right. We should get a move on, don't ya think?" Tobee tried unsuccessfully to lighten the mood.

Andy climbed up onto Boo's muddy back without a word. They set off at a brisk pace - watching the sky through the trees and warily listening for any strange noises. They stayed in the shadow of the forest – away from any open areas.

Andy was amazed at how the horse could find her way through the dark with only the occasional consultation with Tobee. He was also impressed with Tobee's memory. The travel instructions from the King had obviously involved a lot of detail. Whenever Boo asked a question about which direction to go next, Tobee didn't hesitate with the answer. Andy figured that faeries would need to have well trained memories to remember all the magic spells they used.

At dawn, they found themselves at the base of a steep, rugged mountain. They stopped and stared up at the peak as the sun slowly rose.

"Sorry guys," Boo stood with hanging head and droopy ears. "I just have to take a break. Every step just seems to get harder. Must be something about this place," she looked around with weary eyes.

Glancing at each other, Tobee and Andy both felt a prick of fear and concern. It had been obvious that Boo was getting weaker by the hour. But she never complained about it. Now, besides looking exhausted, she was admitting that she was drained.

"Uh, okay. We'll just go eat over there and let you rest," Tobee pointed to a large rock. "Just call us when you're ready to go."

Boo nodded and dropped to her belly, asleep before her

muzzle touched the ground.

After shrinking Andy, Tobee brought out the rest of the food that he had packed. Somber now, their thoughts on Boo's failing strength, they ate in silence. After a brief rest, the boys quickly grew bored and wandered off through the forest.

"T-t-t-tag, you're it!" Andy slapped Tobee on the back and took off at a sprint.

Within seconds, Tobee poked him on the shoulder and zipped ahead.

"Hey, that's ch-ch-cheating!" shouted Andy.

He dashed around a tree trunk and slid to a halt inches from Tobee's rigid body. They were at the edge of a small, devastated meadow. Holes of various sizes pocketed the glen. The ground was blackened as if a flash fire had been through the area. The surrounding forest, usually alive with the sound of chirping birds, was quiet. Not a hint of a breeze rustled the tops of the trees. Just silence. And an unshakeable feeling of dread.

Chapter 9

"This must be an old Magic Spot," whispered Tobee. "Let's go look down one of the holes."

Before Andy could stop him, Tobee took to the air and hovered above the nearest hole. Left on the ground by himself, Andy anxiously rocked from foot to foot. Tobee disappeared from view as he lowered himself over the edge of the hole for a better look.

Afraid to holler, and even more afraid to be alone, Andy hesitantly made his way to the edge. Scrambling to the lip of the depression, he finally caught sight of Tobee. The faerie was slowly descending into the hole.

"Tobee! Where are you g-g-g-going? Get b-b-b-b-back here!" Andy's hoarse whisper scratched his throat.

Startled, Tobee looked up and lost his balance - falling backwards through the air and hitting the side of the hole. The loose dirt started an avalanche and the faerie was caught in the downward slide. Andy had hauled his upper body over the edge and was grasping for Tobee's outstretched arm when he felt the ground give out beneath him. Head first, he tumbled after Tobee into the pit.

They somersaulted and bounced for several minutes, until they finally came to a sudden bone wrenching stop. Once they realized they weren't moving anymore, their screams of fear subsided. Tobee spat out a mouthful of dirt while Andy rubbed grit from his eyes. After adjusting to the sudden change from bright sunlight to the more subtle light of Tobee's chest, the boys looked around.

Sprawled on the top of a quartz-like pedestal, they were surrounded by darkness. Above them a tiny pinprick of light showed where they had descended from. Speechless and bug eyed, the boys looked at each other in horror.

Andy slowly stood up. On tiptoes, he touched the earth ceiling above them. A shower of dirt cascaded down and threw him onto his back beside Tobee. Spluttering, he looked up and saw the ceiling was still hovering above them. Something invisible was holding the dirt in place.

"Look," whispered Tobee. He pointed his chest light to one side.

The dirt that had fallen on them rolled across the flat top of their platform and disappeared over the side. Belly crawling to the edge, the boys peeked over. Expecting to see a deep chasm surrounding them, they were surprised when all they found was a solid dirt floor.

They lay there, quivering in fear.

"What are we g-g-g-going to do?" murmured Andy.

"I don't know. Wait for Boo to find us?"

"H-h-h-how's she going to f-f-find us d-d-d-down here?"

"We could yell," Tobee suggested.

"She's not g-g-going to hear our v-v-v-voices when we're this size. Besides, w-w-we're under a l-l-l-layer of dirt."

"Well, we can't go up."

The boys looked around them - into the darkness.

"Maybe we should see if we can walk on it," Tobee

gazed over the edge and motioned at the ground beneath them.

"I g-g-guess," Andy muttered hesitantly.

Tobee slowly swung his body around so he was hanging feet first. Andy grabbed his arms and slowly lowered him.

"Whoa, you're really l-l-light," whispered Andy.

"Yeah, I'm a faerie. What did you expect?"

"But how c-c-c-can you carry me if you're so l-l-l-light?" Andy, totally distracted by this realization, lifted Tobee up and down with ease.

"You don't have to be heavy to be strong." Irritated now, Tobee slapped at Andy's hands. "Now come on, let me go."

"Oh. R-r-right. Sorry," whispered Andy.

Tobee daintily touched the ground. When nothing happened, he put his full weight on his feet.

"It seems okay," Tobee jumped up and down. The floor was solid beneath his feet.

Andy slipped over the edge and found that it held him as well.

"Okay, n-n-n-now what?"

"Um….. we look for a way out?" Tobee tried to sound confident.

Andy worriedly glanced back up at their entrance point.

"I g-g-guess…"

With Tobee's chest light showing the way, they tentatively made their way through the darkness. Trying to keep as straight a line as possible, they kept their backs to the crystal pedestal. Every once in a while, Tobee would turn around and shine his light at the platform. Light reflected back, reassuring them of their direction.

The roof above varied in height. At times, they had to stoop to prevent brushing their heads along the surface and sending down a shower of dirt. At other times, it was several inches above them.

Tobee spread his wings and tried to fly but to no avail. He was very upset by this. To a faerie, being able to fly was as natural as talking. Faeries were not courageous by nature. They were a peaceful species and rather shy and timid in unfamiliar circumstances. If they felt threatened by something, they would take flight. Not being able to fly made Tobee feel helpless and vulnerable.

"It's okay. It's j-j-just this p-p-p-place," Andy put his hand on the faerie's shoulder and tried to console him. "As s-s-soon as we g-g-g-get out of here, I'm sure your w-w-w-wings will work again."

Eventually they found walls on each side of them, gradually narrowing into a passageway.

"Must be a tunnel," muttered Tobee.

"What if there are t-t-t-tunnels all over. H-h-h-how do we know which one t-t-t-to take? And we c-c-c-can hardly see the p-p-platform anymore," Andy worried as he glanced behind them.

"Yeah, but what else are we going to do. This tunnel must have been made by something....Right?"

"I guess," mumbled Andy.

With Tobee in the lead, and the pedestal no longer in sight, the boys slowly followed the narrow, winding tunnel.

Chapter 10

Sniff. Sniff. Sniff.

Tobee stopped so abruptly that Andy ran into the back of him.

"What?"

"*SHHHHH*! I just heard something." Tobee's quivering whisper sent chills up Andy's spine.

"It sounded like something was sniffing." This time Tobee murmured right into Andy's ear. Rigidly, they stood side by side, gripping each other's arms.

Sniff. Sniff. Sniff.

They gasped and in their haste to turn and run, fell over each other and landed in a heap on the tunnel floor. Before they could scramble to their feet, they heard a squeaky voice emerge from the darkness.

"No, no, no. Stay right where you are."

Tobee spun around and the beam from his chest light landed on a cluster of eight yellow eyes. The eyes disappeared immediately, accompanied by a distressed squeak.

"Ow, ow, ow. That's bad. Ooooooh."

Andy and Tobee slowly stood up – staring at the spot where they had seen the eyes. They inched forward. All they could hear was whimpering and sniveling. Out of the dark emerged a strange looking creature. It squirmed and wiggled out of the light beam. Tobee felt enough sympathy for the creature to turn his light to the side. But not before they had a good look at it.

Translucent skin showed a web of veins under the surface. Six legs on each side of its oblong body had toes shaped like rounded hoes. Its head consisted of its many eyes – all squished shut against the light – and a round mouth that was pursed tight in frustration. Above the eyes protruded two spindly antennas that must have also held eyes. They were quivering and bending this way and that to avoid the light.

When Tobee turned his chest away from the creature, it stopped its squirming and whimpered, "Good, good, good. Stay like that. Ohhhh, my poor eyes."

A moment of silence was followed by a chorus of three nervous voices all asking, "Who are you?"

A heartbeat of startled silence passed and then all three burst into nervous giggles. Andy and Tobee, so relieved to not be in danger (who could feel threatened by such a feeble, wimpy character) slapped each other on the back. Their giggles turned into guffaws. The creature, standing in the shadows, had a strange sort of laugh – a series of blubbery lip flutters.

Finally, nervous tension spent, the boys peered into the shadows to have a better look at the creature. It, in turn, sized them up with all ten eyes. Its antennas moved up and down - viewing them from head to toe. The eyes blinked independently - every second there was one eye closing while the rest gazed at the boys. Andy was mesmerized by the constant blinking. He found himself trying to guess which eye would blink next.

"So, so, so," it began. "What are you doing in my tunnel?"

"Uh… we kind of fell through a hole," Tobee pointed behind him.

"Oh, yes, yes, yes. I was worried about that. Ever since my egg was stolen, the roof has been loose," the creature whined.

Silence followed. Tobee poked the spellbound Andy in the ribs to get his attention.

"Ouch!" Andy pushed Tobee on the shoulder, "Tch, geez."

"It said '*egg*'. Do you think it was a Thunderegg?" whispered Tobee.

"I d-d-don't know. Maybe."

"Well, what do we do?"

Andy peered back into the shadows. "Um….. C-c-c-c-could you tell us how to g-g-g-g-get out of here?"

"Oh, yes, yes, yes. Come this way."

The creature started backing down the tunnel. As the boys started to follow, Tobee inadvertently pointed his light at the creature.

"Ahhh, no, no, no," it squealed.

"Whoa, sorry!"

The boys stopped in mid stride as Tobee swung around and stood behind Andy, blocking the light.

"How are we g-g-g-going to see where we're g-g-going if we don't have light?"

The creature's backwards scuffling was growing quieter as it disappeared down the dark tunnel. The boys, growing panicky, started to follow.

"Ouch!" Andy walked into the side of the tunnel.

"Oomph!" Tobee walked into Andy and they slid down

the crumbling wall to the floor.

"Wait! Why don't you use the Thunderegg? Maybe its light won't bother ....that thing."

Andy dug out the bag holding his Thunderegg and opened it. Immediately, the tunnel was filled with light. They jumped to their feet and started to jog after the creature. Twisting and turning, the passageway continued on with the strange creature no where in sight. Eventually, they passed sections of wall that were made of bark.

"Huh," puffed Tobee. "These look like tree trunks. We must be under the forest."

"Where d-d-d-did that thing go?" panted Andy. "How c-c-c-can it move so fast – b-b-backwards?"

The boys continued their pursuit, winding around and over tree roots that protruded through the walls of the tunnel.

Finally, the narrow tunnel walls started to widen. Slowing down, they looked from left to right, searching for the missing tunnel owner.

The passageway opened up into a large cave. In the middle stood not one, but two creatures - identical to the one they stumbled across in the tunnel. They stood side by side. Twenty eyes watching and blinking.

The cave smelled like a dried up swamp. Covering their mouths and noses with their hands, the boys slowly approached the twins.

"I guess the Thunderegg's light doesn't bother them," commented Tobee in a whisper.

"Up, up, up. That's the way out," the antenna eyes pointed up.

"Okay. Thanks," Tobee replied.

Curious, Andy asked, "What h-h-h-happened to your

egg?"

"Tch, tch, tch," the mouths muttered. "Badness took it. Dug right down and scooped it." The eyes looked sad and forlorn, antennas drooping.

"We miss it. Don't know what to do." A big sigh. "We're the guards, you see. It's *our* egg." Now the creature was getting sulky and a bit angry.

"Bad, bad, bad. We need it back." The eyes had a crazed, desperate look in them.

Suddenly, two sets of antennas stood up rigidly, eyes focused on Andy's Thunderegg. All twenty eyes stopped blinking.

"Ooooooooh, my, my, my," identical mouths whispered in unison. "What do we have here?" Its voice took on a silky, sly quality that made Andy's skin crawl. The creature started to slither towards them.

"Uh oh," whispered Andy.

Remembering the King's warning about keeping the Thunderegg hidden, he quickly doused the light. Tobee's light, no longer hidden behind the Thunderegg's, shot straight at the creature's faces.

"Argh!"

As the heads spun away from each other in unison, avoiding the light, Andy and Tobee gasped. It wasn't twins they were looking at. It was one creature with two heads! Its oblong, wormy body had a head on each side. It scuttled to the far wall as Tobee slowly advanced towards it.

"Tell us how to get out of here, or I'll keep coming," warned the faerie.

Andy was impressed. He could tell that Tobee was as nervous as he was, but he put on a brave face and threatening voice. The creature was blinded by the light and in obvious discomfort.

"Okay, okay, okay. Just go up," it whimpered.

"WHERE do we go up?" Tobee growled in frustration.

"There, there, there," the antennas, eyes squished shut, pointed behind the boys, at the centre of the room.

Andy swung around as Tobee backed up. A tree root hung from the ceiling. Andy could see a wide crack hidden in the shadows. He stepped inside and looked up. High above, he could see a pinprick of light.

"I th-th-think it goes up the middle of the t-t-tree."

"How do we get up there?" Tobee's voice quivered.

Andy looked back towards the creature and saw it advancing towards them, a few of the braver eyes blinking and squinting against the light.

Andy felt around and found a narrow path worn into the tree that spiraled up the trunk.

"Come on," shouted Andy. "Stay c-c-close to the edge and follow the p-p-path up." He grabbed Tobee's arm and hauled him through the crack.

They ran – uphill - as fast as they could. Whenever the scrabbling sounds of the creature got too close, Tobee would spin around and shine his light on its face. If he could surprise it, it would fall off the pathway and have to start its journey over again.

Panting, sweating and with hearts pounding, the boys finally emerged from the darkness of the hollow tree. They ran onto a branch, high above the ground.

"Whoa," shouted Andy as he came to an abrupt halt. He stood on the edge of the branch, teetering back and forth - arms wind-milling as he tried to catch his balance.

Without thinking, Tobee grabbed one of Andy's flailing

arms and jumped into the air. They hovered there, both heaving a sigh of relief.

"See! We just had t-t-to get out of there. I knew your w-w-wings would work again," exclaimed Andy, a huge smile of relief lighting up his face.

Tobee spun around when they heard scrambling coming from behind them. Not waiting around to see what sunlight would do to the creature's sensitive eyes, they zipped off into the forest.

Chapter 11

When they finally found Boo, she was in a full blown panic. Covered in sweat, whites of her eyes flashing, she had dug up the ground running back and forth searching for them. Finally, after they had told their story and Boo was convinced they were unharmed, she stopped her pacing. She slowly approached them, lowered her head and pinned them with her large angry brown eyes.

"You boys MUST think before you act. I know you believe this is all one exciting adventure, but there is real danger here. If anything had happened to either one of you ..." A pained look flashed across her face before she continued. "Well, we won't go there. Look," she continued more patiently, "I know this is a huge responsibility. It would be for an adult, let alone young boys. But for some reason you two have been chosen. Wizards and Kings know more about these kinds of things than we do so we must trust them. "

"Sorry," mumbled the boys in unison. Heads hanging, they kicked at the dirt in front of them.

After a short rest, the trio started their journey up the mountain. Tobee tried to convince Boo that he and Andy should go on ahead. She could wait at the bottom of the mountain for their return. Boo wouldn't even consider it. She felt it was her responsibility to see the boys safely delivered to Kailani - especially after their latest escapade. The climb ahead of her was going to be draining but she would take the time to rest later. They managed to persuade her to let Andy remain faerie size so Tobee could carry him. She'd be relieved of his weight and they'd make better time.

There was a faint trail that zigzagged up the mountain but it was still tough going. The underbrush was thick and the footing was loose. Boo scrabbled her way up a few steps at a time. She was soon dripping with sweat and covered with scratches.

Tobee and Andy flitted from branch to branch. They ducked under jagged tree boughs and skirted around bramble bushes. At one point Andy insisted on being brought back to size so he could carry his own weight. He thought it might help Boo if they were beside her, encouraging her on. This didn't last long. He slowed them down considerably.

Hour after hour they trudged up the steep mountain. Trees gradually gave way to rocks. This made the footing for Boo even more treacherous and without the protection of the trees, the trio was buffeted by the wind. It got worse the higher they climbed. Tobee's delicate wings were no match for the unpredictable gusts. He and Andy made slings out of Boo's mane and hung from her neck, out of the wind.

After another brief rest, they took their bearings and saw an ancient, leafless tree near the peak of the mountain. Tucked between two branches near the top of the tree was a huge nest.

Boo, gasping for air with head and ears drooping, told the boys to continue on - she could go no further.

"Aww Boo, we c-c-can't leave you here."

Andy was concerned about leaving her. She had been with him for this whole dream. Her size and strength and confidence had been a great comfort to him. Now, she was weak and spent. He felt it was his turn to take care of her.

"No, Andy. I just can't go on." Her voice was faint and she shook all over. It was obvious she was past the point of exhaustion. "You have to go without me. I'll be fine after I rest. I'll stay right here until you get back."

Reluctantly, Andy agreed. He gave her drooping neck a gentle hug then turned to Tobee.

"Okay, l-l-let's get this over with."

Tobee charmed Andy back to normal size then crawled inside the front pocket of his hoodie. Andy scrambled up the sharp, rocky slope as carefully as he could. Every time they glanced down the mountain, Boo was watching them. She encouraged them with a nod of her head. Her whinnies were carried away in the wind.

Finally, they reached the base of the tree. Andy, exhausted, dropped down and leaned against the rough, grey trunk. When he could finally breathe normally, he asked Tobee, "Okay, h-h-how are we supposed to g-g-get up to the nest?"

"Well, the tree is blocking the wind on this side, so if we fly up here, we won't get blown back down the mountain." Tobee pointed out a route he had in mind.

When they finally reached the bottom of the nest, they stopped. They heard rustling and a faint cooing sound coming from the depths of the eagle's nest.

Very slowly the boys climbed the braided branches of the nest wall and peaked over the edge.

At first the wind was so strong they had a hard time opening their eyes. Suddenly, the wind was blocked. They opened their eyes and gasped. They were staring at their own reflections. Blinking, they took in the larger picture. An inch from their faces was a huge, angry golden eye. Surrounding the eye was a large bird's head. With a swoop and a rustle of feathers the eagle stood up, wings spread wide. She screamed and pounced on them. Her vicious yellow curved beak missed them both as they swung away from her attack. She stretched to her full height. Her wing span was wider than the huge nest.

"WAIT! KAILANI! KING FERBINSOL SENT US," bellowed Tobee.

She stopped her attack in mid lunge. Slowly, she folded her wings and lowered her body. The fierce eyes blinked once.

"Kailani?" whispered Andy.

She tilted her head.

"Are you K-k-k-kailani?" he repeated.

"Who asks?" she spat out.

"I'm Andy - a D-d-dreamer. King Ferbinsol said y-y-you could help us. I n-n-n-need to get to the G-g-gemstone Wizard."

She shrugged her wings closer to her body. And glared menacingly at Andy.

"And why should I help you?" she sneered.

Tobee piped up. "King Ferbinsol thinks that Andy can help fix the magic in Dreamland."

At that, Kailani drooped. She lost her menacing glare and threatening stance. Turning to the side, she peered at what lay on the other side of the nest. The boys snuck a peak between her legs. There were three eggs lying together. They were carefully tucked into a soft downy bed of feathers and grass. None were in the process of hatching. As a matter of fact, they all looked cold - and dead.

Kailani's sadness was evident. She gently nudged the eggs. It was like she was willing them to reveal the young life inside. She sighed and snuggled her body over them to protect and warm them.

The boys looked at each other, shrugged and slowly crawled over the edge of the nest. They settled into the downy softness and waited, watching the bird tend to her eggs.

Andy woke up to a gentle cooing. He elbowed Tobee awake and pointed towards Kailani. She was tenderly covering the eggs with the soft bedding. When she was satisfied they were as protected as possible, she turned to the boys.

"I'll take you," she nodded towards Andy. "But only you." She turned her piercing glare on Tobee. "You'll stay here and watch over…," she stopped and glanced back towards the eggs, "…them."

Tobee, eyes huge with fright, nodded. The boys didn't have a chance to say anything to each other. When Andy was instructed to climb onto the eagle's back, his jaw dropped. Tobee saw his hesitation and realized his friend's fear of heights was rearing its ugly head.

"Count. Just count," Tobee whispered. "You'll be fine."

Andy flashed him a watery smile, took a deep breath and climbed onto the huge bird's back.

Kailani stepped up onto the rim of the nest and dropped over the edge.

The flight was cold. And fast. They flew over snow covered mountains and green valleys interlaced with blue ribbons of rivers. Whole forests zipped by below them. When they flew lower, Andy watched in awe as rivers with cascading waterfalls, quiet lakes and meadows populated by wildflowers zoomed beneath. His fear of heights was forgotten.

In contrast to the beautiful scenery below, they passed over several areas that had been burned and dug out. Andy assumed that these were more Magic Spots. He shivered as he remembered the strange, double headed wormy creature they had encountered.

Day turned to night. It got colder. The starless night sky only added to Andy's total discomfort and terror. He gripped the feather shafts so tight, his hands went numb.

Finally, he figured out how to burrow under the feathers to borrow warmth from Kailani's body. He closed his eyes to the total blackness of the night. There was no time to think of anything besides hanging on and trying to stay warm.

At dawn, they landed at the edge of a meadow. Andy stiffly slipped off of the eagle's back. When he turned towards her, she stretched her wings and hovered over him. The eagle took a deep breath and blew on him. Instantly, Andy grew to his human size. He gasped and looked down at Kailani.

Before he could ask any questions, she said, "The little dragon is there." She motioned towards a cave opening half way up the mountain on the other side of the meadow.

"He'll show you where to go."

With that, she was off - turning a circle in the air before flying back in the direction they had come from.

Andy was alone for the first time. He was tired. He was hungry. And he felt totally overwhelmed by this strange world. Squatting in the grass, he stared up at the cave. There were a few trees and bushes near the opening. Otherwise, it was a rough, rocky area. There was no movement or sound anywhere close to the opening.

"A d-d-dragon?" Andy muttered to himself. His eyes widened as he realized what Kailani had said. "No way!" He groaned and fell back onto the grass surrounding him - eyes squished shut.

Andy woke up when the sun was high. Thankful for the

warmth, he laid still for a few more minutes. He pulled his Thunderegg out of his pocket and turned it over in his hands. It was purple. It really was a beautiful thing, thought Andy. He had a feeling it wouldn't be his much longer. With a resigned sigh, he pulled himself up and looked towards the cave.

"I might as well g-g-get on with it."

With the Thunderegg once again tucked safely away in his pocket, Andy started off.

When he finally reached the far side of the meadow, he lost sight of the cave. Trees climbed up the side of the mountain, hiding anything on the other side. He zigzagged his way up, hoping that when he came out of the forest he would be close to the cave. The climb was not as steep or rough as the climb to Kailani's nest and it didn't take him nearly as long as he thought it would. When he emerged from the forest, the dark opening was a stone's throw away.

Chapter 12

Andy slowly approached the cave. He tried to muffle his footsteps by walking on the sparse grassy patches. The opening was huge. He was just about to step over the dirt threshold, when a strange blowing sound echoed its way out of the cave. Andy spun around and hid behind a stumpy bush. The same sound was heard over and over again. Tired of waiting, he slithered through the doorway and hid in the shadows. One more breathy snort was heard and then a scuffling sound. It became louder as something approached from the depths of the darkness. Shaking with fright, Andy slowly inched farther into the shadows. The scuffling was soon accompanied by an irritated grumbling noise. Andy watched as a huge shadow became visible on the far wall. As the noises became louder, the shadow grew. His eyes widened and his breath came in gasps as he realized he was looking at a shadow of a large dragon. Andy held his breath as the shadow left the sunny wall of the cave. The monster would be visible at any second. Andy was just about to slink farther into the shadows when out from the dark walked the strangest sight he had ever seen.

Waddling towards the cave entrance was a stubby creature that looked like it belonged in a comic book. No taller than Andy's shoulder, it had huge golden eyes framed with long eyelashes. Its body was speckled with so many colors Andy figured it just couldn't decide what color to be.

Between its large floppy ears was a spiky tuft of hair. It looked like it had swallowed a large basketball because its pot belly stuck straight out. The stumpy tail swung to and fro with each shuffling step. When Andy saw the tiny wings, he couldn't help but snort. He thought of Tobee and knew he would have had a good chuckle if he'd been there. Those wings would embarrass a faerie, let alone a dragon!

Just as Andy clamped his hand over his mouth, realizing his mistake, the creature threw up its arms and screeched. Andy, in turn, started howling. The sounds echoed and reverberated off the cave walls, making it sound like there was an army of creatures screaming through the cave towards them. Both of them made a dash for the entrance. Andy tripped and fell just as he reached the opening. The dragon fell over him and went tumbling into the bushes. It quickly hauled itself to its feet and launched into a tirade.

"What the heck are you doin'? Thith ith my houthe and you jutht come in without knockin'? Geeth! Ya jutht about gave me a heart attack." He put his hands on his round hips and glared down his stubby snout at the intruder.

Andy stood up and brushed off his pants.

"Uh, sorry. I was j-j-just a little surprised to s-s-see you," stammered Andy. When the dragon continued to tap his clawed foot on the ground and look him up and down, Andy continued.

"Um, K-k-k-kailani just…"

"What! Kailani'th here? Where? Thee never cometh here anymore." He spun wildly in circles, searching the sky.

"No no. She l-l-l-left me way over there." Andy pointed towards the trees below. "I w-w-w-walked the rest of the way."

"Oh….Oh, well." The dragon was clearly disappointed. "I uthed to get company coming all the time – ya know –

going to the cathle and thtuff." He sighed. "Now Ernie ith the only one I ever thee anymore."

"Ernie?" Andy replied weakly.

"Yup, he'th my neighbor. Hmmm, come to think of it, I don't even know where he livth." He stood there, deep in thought, scratching his scruffy chin.

"Huh." He brought his attention back to Andy. "Tho, my name ith Thpike."

"Thpike?"

"No, Thpike. Ya know, with an eth."

Andy cocked his head. "Spike?"

"Yup, thpike. Pleathed ta meet ya." He waddled over to shake hands. Andy cautiously took the dragon's taloned claw in his and shook. Before Andy could introduce himself, Spike changed the subject again.

"Ya wanna thee my houth? It'th pretty big, ya know," he spun around and started to waddle back to the cave entrance. "The Withard thaid I'd grow into it, but, well.....nothin'th happened yet."

Andy shook his head at Spike's low attention span.

"I really n-n-need to get to the G-g-g-gemstone Wizard."

The dragon looked at Andy with suspicion, "Hmmmm. You're a Dreamer, right?"

"Yeahhhhh," mumbled Andy.

"Tho, why do you want to thee the Withard? Dreamerth never vithit the Withard. He doethn't like to be bothered, ya know." The dragon pulled up to his full height and stuck out his chest. He obviously took his job seriously, feeling protective about the Wizard's privacy.

Andy sighed. He was going to have to tell his story

AGAIN. Before he could get started, there was a rustling in the bushes nearby.

Spike swung around and exclaimed, “Ernie! Howth it goin?”

Andy’s eyebrows shot into the air and he stumbled backwards - away from the large mud colored snake that slithered out from under the bushes.

“Hey Spike. Who’s this guy?” Ernie hissed as he rattled his tail towards Andy.

Heart pounding, Andy slowly and carefully straightened up. He glanced at Spike who seemed to be quite at ease around the menacing, slimy snake.

“Uh, m-m-m-my name’s Andy.” He mumbled when Spike swung back around with questioning eyes.

Spike looked at Ernie and explained that Andy had come to see the Gemstone Wizard. Ernie uncoiled part of his long body and slowly advanced towards Andy.

“Oh really.” As he looked Andy up and down with his piercing yellow eyes, he continued, “And what would you want with the Wizard?”

Andy felt an immediate dislike towards Ernie and had no intention of telling him about the Thunderegg.

“He’s expecting m-m-m-me….”

Before Andy could continue, Spike interrupted.

“The Withard’th expecting you? Geeth, why didn’t you thay tho!” Spike grabbed his arm and headed along a path through the bushes. “Come on, then. I’ll thow you where to go. Thee ya, Ernie.”

Ernie narrowed his eyes, hissed and slithered back under the bush.

They started hiking along the mountain trail with Andy

glancing behind him every few steps. He couldn't get rid of the feeling that he was being watched.

It was slow going since Spike waddled at a very leisurely pace. And he was such a chatter box. Andy had a hard time getting a word in. The main topic of conversation was that Spike was trying to learn how to fly.

"Ernie keepth telling me I'll never do it, but I will. Jutht wait and thee."

"S-s-s-s-so, how did you m-m-m-meet Ernie?" Andy couldn't understand how Spike felt comfortable around the snake. There was such a menacing and threatening air about him.

"He thowed up one day – after everybody thtopped coming. And he'th the only guy that ever cometh around anymore. That'th kind of weird, ithn't it?" Spike dwelled on this thought for a moment before he continued chattering.

Eventually, he stopped and pointed down the path to where it divided into an upper and lower route.

"Tho, to get to the Withard'th cathle, you jutht have to follow the higher path. It goeth around the mountain and cometh to a valley. You'll thee the cathle in the middle of a meadow."

"You can't come with m-m-me?" Andy tried not to sound panicky.

"Nope. I gotta thtay on thith thide of the mountain. I'm the gate keeper for the Withard, ya thee. Not that he getth much company any more…." Spike's voice dwindled off, his head tilted to the side.

Andy cleared his throat.

"Yeah, tho," Spike continued. "Jutht follow that path and you'll find the cathle."

"Oh. Okay. Th-th-thanks." Andy sighed and looked

down the trail before turning back to the dragon.

"No problem. I'll thee ya on your way back." He started to waddle back down the path. "Thay 'hi' to the Withard for me and tell him I'll be flying thoon." He waved and with a flutter of his useless wings, disappeared down the path.

Andy ran his fingers through his hair and looked at the path ahead of him. With a groan, he started down the trail.

An hour passed uneventfully. As he entered a barren, rocky area the feeling that something or someone was watching him became more intense. He started to glance warily over his shoulder every few steps. Walking turned into a slow jog. The trail twisted and turned around boulders and blackened bushes. He kicked up dust as he went, so the trail behind him became hazy. Sliding to a stop, he spun around when he heard a quiet hissing in a bush he had just passed. He stopped and with a growing feeling of dread, watched Ernie slither out from behind the brambly bush.

"How d-d-d-did you get here so f-f-f-fast," whispered Andy.

"Oh, we snakes can travel quickly," he hissed. Then he demanded, "Where's Spike?"

"He went b-b-b-back home. I know the w-w-w-way now. See you around."

Andy turned, intending to make a hasty get away but was blocked when Ernie swung his tail across Andy's path.

"I'm going to show you a shortcut. If you keep following this path, you won't get there until after dark. You don't want to travel around here in the dark now, do you?"

Ernie's hiss took on a singsong tone as he tried to sound convincing. But Andy wasn't fooled. He looked down the path and saw that it disappeared around a large boulder. All he could see in the distance were more rocks.

"Spike t-t-t-told me to stick to the p-p-p-path." Andy's heart was beating so hard, he was sure it would jump out of his chest. He just wanted to run, but the large, menacing snake was slowly creeping closer and closer to him, blocking his way.

Ernie's voice softened. He inched closer to Andy and stared into his eyes.

"Little Spike doesn't know the mountain like I do. Come on. All you have to do is go through a short tunnel. Then you'll be on the other side. The Wizard's castle will be right there."

As Andy stared into Ernie's eyes, he felt his mind numbing. No matter how hard he tried to move his body, nothing happened. He was frozen. He couldn't seem to look away from Ernie's eyes.

"You don't want to keep the Wizard waiting now, do you?" Ernie hissed. His forked tongue wiggled inches away from Andy's face.

Slowly, Ernie maneuvered his long body around Andy. As he crowded the hypnotized boy against the boulder, he continued. "Just go around this rock. You'll see the cave entrance. Go inside and follow it to the end."

Andy felt his body turn, even though his mind screamed at his muscles to run in the opposite direction. He squeezed around the boulder and sure enough, there was a cave entrance. As he blinked into the darkness he felt his body become his own again. With a gasp, he spun around. As he tried to squeeze back through the opening he came face to face with Ernie's vicious hissing mouth and angry eyes. Gasping with fright, Andy jumped back into the darkness and ran several steps into the tunnel.

Chapter 13

Sweat popped out on his forehead and his heart raced. He was starting to feel nauseous because he couldn't see anything. He rubbed his eyes to no avail. It was pitch black. All he could hear was his own breathing. Looking back one last time towards the entrance, he groaned. He had to choose between the unknown of the dark tunnel or facing the sinister snake. After a silent debate, he pulled the black bag out of his pocket. When he opened it the light from the shining rock almost blinded him. Glancing one last time at the cave entrance, Andy inched forward into the darkness.

The tunnel was about a foot taller than he was and just as wide. With perfectly smooth walls and floor and semi circular shape, Andy imagined an underground river had once run through it.

He stopped for a break and sat against the cool wall of the tunnel. His heart had stopped its wild beating the farther he traveled from Ernie and the entrance.

Sitting in the small pool of light that the Thunderegg emitted, Andy realized how lonely he felt. He thought of Tobee and Boo and realized how much easier it was to digest the strangeness of this world when he had company. Talking horses and little faeries were strange guides, he thought. But he missed their company and humor.

Twangs of homesickness weighed heavy on his heart as

his thoughts drifted to his mom and Brian. Once again he worried about his mom's reaction to his sleeping body in the car. How many days had it been now? He'd lost track. His mom had gone through so much hardship and heartache since his dad died. Feeling terrible about being the cause for more worry, he sighed. He realized there was really nothing he could do but get the Thunderegg to the Gemstone Wizard as quickly as possible.

As he was getting ready to leave his rest spot, he heard a very faint whirring sound. Immediately his heart started to thump. He quickly dowsed the Thunderegg's light by dropping it into the black bag. Andy stood up in the darkness, ready to run. He held his breath and listened to the sound become louder. His head swiveled back and forth. He couldn't figure out if the sound was coming from behind him or in front of him. All of a sudden, a tiny light revealed itself from the tunnel he had just passed through. It came closer and closer. Shivering with fear, Andy sunk to the ground. The light stopped and hovered above Andy's head.

"Geez Andy! This is not the time to play hide and seek!" said Tobee in a disgusted voice.

"Tobee?!" Andy gasped. "H-h-how did you get here? M-m-man, you scared me to d-d-death!" Andy stood up and scooped Tobee out of the air.

"Whoa! Careful there big guy! You're gonna squish a wing," Tobee laughed as Andy's over enthusiastic hand-hug took his breath away. "When Kailani came back to her nest she told me to hop on her back. We flew straight here, but it took me awhile to convince that wannabe dragon to let me catch up with you. What is with that guy, anyway? He won't stop talking."

Andy burst into laughter. He was so relieved to see Tobee - if he didn't laugh, he'd cry. And THAT would not do - Tobee would tease him non-stop.

"B-b-b-but, how did you find the t-t-t-tunnel entrance? Ernie - the snake..."

Tobee grimaced. "When I caught up to you, he was forcing you behind the boulder. I had to cast a spell on him before I could follow you in here. Boy, what a creep."

"Yeah," Andy agreed. "Come on. Let's get g-g-going. I just want to g-g-g-get out of this place. Can you p-p-p-point your light down there so I don't f-f-f-fall on my face."

The boys set off down the tunnel with Tobee perched on Andy's shoulder. Their chattering and nervous laughter bounced off the curved stone walls surrounding them.

Finally, the boys emerged from the tunnel into a large cavern. They could tell it was big because their voices echoed off the walls, over and over again. A faint dripping sound could be heard from somewhere in the darkness. The ground was rough and covered with rocks and stones of varying sizes. It smelled worse than the worm's hole - forcing the boys to breath through their mouths to avoid as much of the smell as possible.

After some discussion they decided to walk the perimeter of the cave to look for another tunnel. Ernie had said it would take them to the other side of the mountain. There was a one sided debate on how much they could trust Ernie. In the end, they decided to investigate the cave. Thoughts of returning to face the snake made both boys shiver.

The walls of the cave were irregular and jagged. They had to walk at a much slower pace to avoid bumping into or tripping over stones and rocky protrusions. Tobee chattered away in Andy's ear. They giggled and poked fun at each other.

As Andy was inching his way around a rather large rock, Tobee leaned over and looked down at Andy's feet.

"WHOA!"

“Wh-wh-what?” Andy yipped and jumped back as his heart started pounding.

“You almost fell into that hole,” Tobee pointed down.

Andy kneeled down to have a better look.

“Wow, that was close,” mumbled Tobee.

In front of them was a hole about as wide as a bus. The faerie’s light only showed a few feet down, so the boys dropped some small stones into it to see if they could tell how deep it was. When they didn’t hear any sounds of the stones hitting the bottom, Andy dropped a large rock. A very faint ‘thud’ could be heard echoing up from the depths.

“Huh. That’s....deep.” Andy inched back, away from the edge.

All of a sudden the ground started to vibrate.

“What...?” The boys looked at each other, eyes huge.

There was a moment of silence. Then a loud snorting noise erupted from the recesses of the cave. The air became smoky and Tobee sneezed. The boys held their breaths during another minute of tense silence.

Out of the darkness rolled a huge roar. It was followed by a blinding fireball. Andy and Tobee fell backwards and scrambled behind a large boulder. Tobee immediately started chanting a protection charm. They quivered in the shadows as the ground continued to vibrate.

Another fireball shot past and hit the wall about ten feet from where they hid. And another one - followed by a very angry bellow - hit the wall on the opposite side. Andy chanced a quick look around the rock just as another one lit up the cave. What he saw was scarier than his worst nightmare. On the other side of the gaping hole in the floor was a huge monster. He couldn’t tell the color of it since it was so dark. But he couldn’t miss the evil red eyes. Smoke streamed out of its huge nostrils on the end of a long, warty snout. It was as tall as a two story building, with a long, powerful neck. Short stubby legs stomped the ground in frustration as the monster tried to locate the intruders. Large wings were tucked into its sides and a long tail ridged with spikes ended at a point. Andy gasped and slid back into their hiding place. He described the monster to a still chanting, white faced Tobee.

"Oh, no," mumbled the faerie. "I wonder if that's the thing that flies at night?"

"Wh-wh-what are we going to do?" asked Andy.

"I can't hold this magic much longer – we're gonna have to think of something. As soon as I let the charm go, he's going to see my light," said Tobee.

The fireballs were landing closer and closer to their hiding spot.

"Wh-wh-why don't you c-c-c-climb into my Th-Th-Th-Thunderegg bag?"

Andy pulled the bag out of his pocket. He opened the top and the light from the rock shot out into the darkness. The monster's irritated shuffling and snorting stopped for a second. Then a huge fireball hit the rock that was hiding them. The boys leaped against the cave wall and scrambled away from the scalding stone. Andy shoved the bag back into his pants as they hopped from rock to crevice. Finally they found another large boulder to hide behind. The creature's anger was evident in its howling roars and sporadic fire bursts.

The boys were shaking and panting with fear.

"Okay, s-s-s-s-so he d-d-d-doesn't like light." Andy kept thinking he should pinch himself to wake up from this nightmare. "Now what?"

"Uh, I have an idea," Tobee's voice was quivering. "I'm

going to fly out and act as a decoy." He pointed back towards the tunnel they had just emerged from. "When it comes after me, you run around the edge until you find the exit. Just run until you get out."

"What! N-n-n-no way!" exclaimed Andy. "You can't fly f-f-f-fast enough. It'll hit you with a f-f-f-fireball before you get to the t-t-t-tunnel."

"Andy, there's no other way. You have to get the Thunderegg to the Wizard or Dreamland will never be the same. This is the only way to do it." Tobee took a deep, steadying breath and continued. "Look. You told me about this baseball game that you play in your world. Just throw me as hard as you can...."

"Are you k-k-k-kidding me? Tobee..." Andy was cut off as Tobee zoomed out from behind the rock, chest light blazing.

"TOBEEEEEE," Andy yelled.

The creature stopped its stomping, snorting and fire breathing. Out of the corner of its eye it saw a tiny light flit across the cave. It let loose a terrifying roar and tossed a fireball towards Tobee. Andy watched the faerie's light zigzag its way toward the tunnel. Several more fireballs flew through the air. Each one landed a little closer to the tiny light. Andy knew he should be running in the opposite direction but he was frozen to the spot with fear. A fireball smashed into the cave wall. When the glare from it diminished, Andy couldn't see Tobee's familiar flitting light.

Fear, anguish and anger boiled together and erupted into a, "NOOOOOOOOOOOO!"

He leaped out from behind the rock, holding the blazing Thunderegg high above his head. As he advanced on the dragon, he continued to bellow. The light from the Thunderegg became more intense. Andy felt a pulsing power travel from the Thunderegg to the rest of his body. His throat burned as his voice became more powerful and commanding. A searing sensation in his hand holding the Thunderegg made him wince but he didn't slow down.

The dragon spun around. Blinded by the brilliant light from the Thunderegg, it stumbled backwards. Catching its tail on a rocky protrusion, the monster thundered to the ground.

Andy stomped towards the fallen dragon. He knew if he backed down now, this monster would destroy the rest of Dreamland and all his friends with it. He would *not* let that happen. With no thought of his own safety, Andy kept pressing on.

Later, as he relived this battle, he would wonder about how the Thunderegg had suddenly appeared in his hand. He would wonder about the words he threw at the monster. His stuttering commands to the dragon to back away slowly changed to a steady stream of unfamiliar words. These tumbled from his lips with confidence and strength. From deep within his being, he understood that he was a conduit for the power of an ancient magic.

The pulsing Thunderegg continued to blind and frustrate the dragon. A fireball spun towards Andy but bounced off an invisible shield surrounding him. The dragon clambered to its feet and tried to move away from the advancing light. There was a loud scrabbling sound, a grunt and a huge bellow as the dragon disappeared from sight. Roars echoed on and on until there was nothing but silence. The monster had fallen into the deep pit.

Andy lowered the Thunderegg. His groaning sigh was filled with relief, followed by a shudder. The power subsided, as did the pulsing light. He slowly turned and headed toward the spot where he last saw Tobee's light. The Thunderegg emitted a strong beam but it still took some time before Andy found the fallen faerie.

Tobee's wings were burnt and smoking. His clothes were torn and tattered. He didn't react to Andy's gentle nudge. Worst of all, his chest light was dark. Andy sat beside Tobee's body for a very long time. Tears of grief over the loss of his first real friend streaked his sooty face. Sobs echoed throughout the cave.

Finally, tears spent, Andy mustered the strength to carry on. He gently cradled Tobee's body in one hand with the Thunderegg in the other. He would take Tobee's tiny body back to his family. It was the least he could do. He trudged through the cave, looking for the exit tunnel.

Chapter 14

Andy emerged from the tunnel into bright sunlight. The first thing he did was gently place Tobee on the ground outside of the cave so he could have a better look at him. Nothing had changed. Tobee's body was cold, battered and empty of all life. He looked so much smaller to Andy than when he was flitting around, teasing and joking everyone around him. With shaking hands and tears streaming down his face, Andy carefully placed the tiny fairie's cold, lifeless form inside his hoodie pocket.

Finally, he took stalk of himself. His clothes were torn and dirty. A burn on his wrist - in the shape of a faerie's wing - had blistered. With a deep sigh, he wearily ran his hands through his dusty, matted hair. He looked up with glazed eyes and inspected his surroundings.

The tunnel opening looked over a desolate mountain valley. It looked like a fire had gone through the area. Huge holes were dug into the ground. A few blackened, branchless tree trunks stood at attention. No movement or sound of life could be heard.

In the centre of the valley, surrounded by the dead land, was a castle. Andy blinked. He rubbed his eyes and blinked again. "No, it couldn't be," he whispered to himself. The castle was a replica of the sand castle he and Tobee had built. Moat and medieval city were replaced by burned trees and grass. Otherwise, that was *his* sand castle. Except that in real life, it was huge. The windows were tiny pinpricks. The walls were a soft sand color. And the roofs of the many turrets were black. It was magnificent. The fire had not touched the castle at all. The burnt ground stopped a few feet from the walls.

Andy clamped his jaw shut and without taking his eyes off of the castle, climbed to his feet. With Tobee gently cradled in his pocket, he started towards the fortress.

It took him an hour to reach the castle. And another hour to circle the perimeter. When he first arrived the main doors were closed. After he walked around the castle walls and arrived back at the doors, they were open.

He stood at the entrance. Not a sound could be heard. Nothing moved. With a deep breath, Andy stepped forward. He expected the castle doors to slam shut behind him. Relieved that this was not the case, Andy continued to walk through the silent courtyard. There was a large water fountain in the middle of the yard. It was dry.

He felt his Thunderegg start to pulse so he dug it out of its bag and held it up. A glance at Tobee's body, snuggled in his pocket, told Andy there was still no change in his friend. Sighing, he continued on.

There was a set of stone stairs that led to another doorway. This led into the castle interior. As soon as Andy stepped on to the bottom stair, the doors above swung open. He glanced down at the heated Thunderegg, now swirling excitedly with blue and gold streaks.

Andy slowly climbed the stairs and crossed the threshold. The largest room he could ever have imagined spread out in front of him. It was as large as a baseball field. There were dark, unlit fireplaces at intervals around the perimeter. Long wooden tables and upturned chairs were spread throughout the room. He thought he could see tapestries hanging on the walls, but everything was covered with such a thick layer of dust, he couldn't be sure. Deserted spider webs hung from the ceiling. Andy's footsteps left prints on the dusty floor. A few hallways and sets of staircases led out of the room. Tiny windows placed high up in the walls emitted very little light. It was dismal and lonely.

Not sure where to go next, Andy walked to the centre - footsteps echoing on the stone floor. Without thinking, he held the Thunderegg up and turned in a circle. It pulsed with a greater intensity when he pointed it towards a narrow staircase off in the distance.

"Okay. I guess that's where we go," he mumbled to himself.

The stairs - made of stone - were sunken in the middle. Andy knew this was from centuries of feet climbing up and down. But the castle was empty. Where were all the people? Where was the Wizard? What was he supposed to do if there was no one here? He was deep in thought as he continued to climb. The stairs eventually stopped at a long hallway. He followed this for a while until he came to another set of stairs. These circled around and around, in tight turns.

"Must be climbing up a tower....this is going on forever." Andy stopped in mid step. His red rimmed eyes widened and his jaw dropped. "Hey, I'm not stuttering! Huh?"

He looked at the now tri colored Thunderegg.

" Twinkle, twinkle little star,

How I wonder what you are."

The familiar verse flew out of his mouth in a whisper.

"Up above the world so high...

…how I wonder what you are!"

By the end of the verse, Andy was dancing in circles. Tears streamed down his face. He felt such a turmoil of emotions - devastation over the loss of his dearest friend and joy for himself. Every birthday wish or wishing well penny he'd ever had had been spent on his dream of speaking normally.

"What'll mom say? Hah, she'll probably cry. She always cries when she's happy." He gently hugged Tobee to his chest. Oh, how he wished his friend could hear him.

"It must have been that weird magic in the dragon's cave," he whispered to himself. Puzzled, he shook his head then decided that it didn't matter how it happened, because HE DIDN'T STUTTER ANYMORE!

He continued up the stairs at a run, chattering nonsense just so he could hear himself talk without stuttering. Around and around he went. The Thunderegg became a sparkling rainbow the higher he went.

Finally! The stairs ended at an intricately carved wooden door. As Andy approached, the door silently swung open. Slowly stepping over the threshold, eyes wide and unblinking, Andy peered into the room. Inside the small, round room was an old man. He was hunched over and leaning on a staff. His dull grey robe had no adornments. Long matted hair and beard surrounded his wrinkled, tired face. The Wizard's bright green eyes were a sharp contrast to his failing body. Air wheezed in and out of his chest as he struggled for each breath.

"Ah! You've made it." The Gemstone Wizard spoke very softly.

Andy nodded and started to introduce himself.

"Oh, I know who you are young Dreamer. We've been

waiting for you for a long time. I've watched your journey," he motioned to a table behind him. On the table was a large, cloudy crystal ball. "You've come just in the nick of time."

His gaze dropped to where Andy was cradling Tobee's body. A look of deep sadness filled his eyes. Sighing, he motioned for Andy to place Tobee on the table beside the crystal ball.

"I'm sorry, young lad. There's no time to waste. You must hurry …" he was interrupted by Andy.

"Mr. Wizard, sir.... Could you tell me what is going on......please. I want to know why I'm here. And why I can't get back home. And why Tobee had to d…," Andy's eyes filled with tears as he looked at the floor.

"Didn't Marley explain our plight?"

"Well, I think he did. But something weird happened. I couldn't understand what he was saying. Then, all of a sudden, I'm here. In this world. I'm not supposed to show my Thunderegg to anyone, but when I accidentally do, things happen. A weird double headed worm tried to steal it and a dragon tried to fry me and Tobee...." his eyes teared up again as he looked at his friend's quiet body. His tirade came to a dwindling halt.

"I see," murmured the Wizard. "Come. Sit. I'll tell you a story. Hopefully this will answer your questions. Then we can get on with the task."

The wizard slowly walked to a chair by a window. Andy settled himself on a soft velvet cushion at the Wizard's feet.

"Long ago this land was full of magic and miracles. Dreamers would come to visit all the time. Dreamstones acted as a key to carry them into this world. Their time here would be filled with adventure. They would have experiences that they could only dream of having in your world."

After a few wheezy breaths, he continued.

"They would stay for a short time and then return to their bodies when it was time for them to wake up. And then our magic started to lose strength. We couldn't control it. It became unsafe. A lot of creatures diminished. Creatures like unicorns, mermaids, and elves have disappeared. Dreamers were getting stuck here for longer than they should have been. We didn't know the cause of this until a few years ago. My brother, Marley…" he chuckled at Andy's surprised look. "Yes, Marley the Wizard is my brother. You see, he discovered that the Thundereggs were vanishing. The Thunderegg is the basis of our magic. Without it, our magic ceases to exist. We still don't know who or what has taken them. Magic Spots all over Dreamland have been demolished. Every time a Thunderegg is taken from the land, our magical powers diminish a little more. And with their disappearance, an underlying evil grows stronger. I kept it at bay as long as I could…" He let out a tired sigh and ran a withered hand over his face.

"Anyway, in a last ditch effort, Marley and I conjured up a spell, combined our power and transported him to your world. He remembered hearing our grandfather tell a story about a Thunderegg sent to your world for safe keeping. Marley believed that he could find this Thunderegg and bring it back here. The only problem is that he got stuck in your world. So, the search was on for a Dreamer who had the courage…and sincerity….and trust….to follow through with the journey it would take to bring it here. You see, most Dreamers ride a unicorn. Then they wake up. Or dance with faeries. Then they wake up. Their dreams are focused on experiences for themselves. Dreamers don't usually put aside their own needs and desires to help others. For the Thunderegg to be brought all this way would take a Dreamer many days. And many experiences he, or she, would never have imagined."

Andy nodded his head in agreement as he remembered the things he had done and seen since he arrived in

Dreamland.

"So, we waited. And waited. Everyday that went by proved more of a challenge to keep the evil at bay. My magic is weakening. The creatures of our land are starting to suffer the consequences of this darkness. When my magic is gone and I have nothing left to protect us, our world will be changed for ever." He sighed. It took great effort to bring himself out of his melancholy. "But you are here now. And so is the last Thunderegg."

Andy pulled the Thunderegg out of his pocket. The Wizard's eyes lit up as he saw the glowing rock. The rainbow of colors flashed and pulsed in a frenzied dance.

"The last Thunderegg," he whispered. He closed his eyes and bowed his head in relief and reverence.

Finally, the old Wizard straightened his tired shoulders and said, with determination, "We must get you to the top. It's time to give this Thunderegg back to Dreamland. It's time to put things back in balance. Come. I believe I can muster just enough power to get you up there." He pushed himself out of his chair and moved to the crystal ball.

Chapter 15

The Wizard's chant sounded strange to Andy's ears. Nothing happened for quite awhile. Then, with a blink of an eye, he found himself on a flat topped mountain. He stumbled back at the sudden change of scenery. It was dusk. The light was quickly fading. He spun around and could see for miles and miles. There were valleys and meadows surrounding him. The farther he looked the more land he could see. Snow capped mountains stood majestically in the distance. The panoramic view was incredible. But there wasn't any sign of life. No sound. No movement. It occurred to him that there were no stars in the sky. When he thought back to the many nighttime hours that he had traipsed through the forest, he realized that there were never any stars in the sky. Just an inky blackness.

Andy sat cross legged on the mountain top and stared off into the growing darkness - the Thunderegg cradled in his hands. The Wizard told him he must give the Thunderegg back to Dreamland but he didn't tell him *how* to do it. And Andy didn't think to ask if there was some sort of procedure. Should he just leave it on the top of the mountain? Or roll it down the steep slope? The gemstone was busy flashing all sorts of color hues. It pulsed and twinkled at an ever increasing speed. The burn on his wrist was red and swollen. The throbbing seemed to beat in time with the Thunderegg's light show.

His mind drifted back to when he first arrived in Dreamland. He remembered how his surprise and disbelief quickly turned into curiosity and wonder. From talking horses and hilarious frogs to flying faeries and fire breathing dragons. He shook his head. These creatures belonged in fairy tales. Yet he was living in a world where they existed.

He thought of Boo and Tobee and knew that he had never had such good friends in his own world. They were accepting and supportive of him. Nothing was ever said about his stutter. And he didn't have a chance to be shy. He was too busy trying to figure out the next turn of events. There was no time to feel self conscious.

As he turned the Thunderegg over and over in his hands, his thoughts turned to Tobee. And his father. When his dad died, Andy was very young. He didn't really understand what was going on. One day his father was there. The next day, he was gone. Now, he had lost a friend. It was a different kind of sorrow but sorrow just the same. A heavy burden and guilt settled over him. Knowing that he needed to return the faerie's body to his family and try to explain his death was almost more than he could bear.

Emotions started to bubble in the pit of his stomach. Grief and anger and loneliness broiled together. His breath started coming in gulps and gasps. Tears of frustration rimmed his eyes. Overwhelmed, he leaped to his feet and threw the Thunderegg as far as he could into the black sky. It arched ever higher into the air. As it reached the point where gravity started its pull, the Thunderegg grew brighter. It gathered speed as it descended. The bright light became smaller and smaller the farther it fell. He watched it plummet into the forest below. Once again, he was left in darkness. Several heartbeats passed with no sound or movement detected from his mountain perch.

Finally, out of the depths of the land below came a rolling thunder. The ground started to vibrate. Sparks started jumping from the ground where the Thunderegg had landed. Within moments it turned into a huge fireworks display. Thunder and sounds of explosions increased to a deafening height and distance. The light show erupted into huge flashes of blinding white light. It spread around Andy's mountain until he was completely surrounded. Sparks shot ever higher into the sky. Cowering on the ground, he covered his ears with his trembling hands. His whimpers of fright couldn't be heard over the war of sound and light raging around him. The chaos seemed to last forever.

Slowly, the sounds diminished. The trembling ground became stable once again. When everything was quiet, Andy opened his eyes. He squinted against the light. It was nighttime but the light emanating from above lit everything below. Andy looked up and gasped in awe. The sky was covered with a blanket of sparkling stars. There were so many that their accumulated light was as intense as the light from a full moon. Falling from the sky was a fine, glittery dust. As his eyes followed the path of the dust towards the ground below him, he saw the forest and land below was intact. There were no gaping holes or burned trees. With all the thunder, explosions and earth shaking he was sure there would have been some damage. When the shimmering dust settled on the ground, it disappeared. His eyes were drawn to something glittering in the meadow below him. The Wizard's castle shimmered in the starlight. A pulsing power emanated from the walls.

"Wow," Andy whispered.

He sighed and dropped his head into his hands. So, this was it. He had done what he was supposed to do. Dreamland would survive. Its magic was restored. He was relieved. And exhausted. Slowly, he lowered himself to the ground. As he stared into the sparkling night sky, his eyelids became heavier and heavier. It wasn't long before he fell into a deep, exhausted sleep.

Chapter 16

Andy woke up slowly to the happy chirping and cooing of birds in a nearby tree. The bright cloak of stars still hung but the sky was getting brighter as the sun rose. He sat up and rubbed his face. Relief mixed with weariness made Andy feel sluggish. His hands dropped to his knees as he sighed. He nearly gave in to the temptation to curl up into a ball and drift back into the oblivion of sleep. But he knew his time in Dreamland was coming to an end. It was time to go home. He puffed out his cheeks and blew out slowly in an attempt to wake himself up.

Just as he was about to stand up, he saw something sparkle on the ground by his foot. Blinking the sleep out of his eyes, Andy slowly reached out and grasped the object that caught his attention. Rolling it back and forth between his thumb and middle finger, it took him a moment before his still sluggish brain told him that the object in question was a piece of the Thunderegg. Andy jumped to his feet. The pulsing rainbow of color was the size of his thumbnail. It merrily twinkled in the palm of his hand.

"Hah! Awesome," he said to himself. As he stuffed it in the black velvet bag, he noticed the burn on his wrist. It wasn't swollen or sore anymore but remained as a red wing shaped scar. He gently ran his finger over the mark and thought of Tobee. The scar was the same size and shape as one of Tobee's wings. With a sad smile, Andy realized that he had a permanent reminder of his dear friend.

He followed the winding path from the top of the mountain to the valley below. When he finally arrived at the castle gates, Andy stopped in mid stride - mouth agape. The transformation was incredible. It was no longer a quiet, dismal place. The castle was bustling with activity. Creatures of all shapes and sizes were in the courtyard. There was laughter and happy chattering. Monkeys splashed in the fountain. Birds zipped to and fro, building nests in lush trees that weren't there before.

When he entered the castle, he didn't recognize the room. The fireplaces hosted warm, crackling fires. Tables and chairs that were once scattered and dusty were polished to a fine sheen and were lined up in long rows. Huge colorful tapestries - each telling a different story - hung from the walls. The room was filled with bustling creatures. Faeries and elves were placing food on tables. Funny looking two headed creatures were shouting directions to no one in particular. Two young unicorns - one black and one golden - were having a friendly jousting match with their horns. Birds hung long ribbons of colorful fabric from the ceiling.

He slowly walked through the crowd, eyes huge in fascination. As he passed, those around him stopped and bowed. He heard whispers of '*…the Chosen One…*' and '*….that's him…*' Andy ducked his head and blushed at the attention.

He quickly found the staircase to the Wizard's tower and started the ascent. A cloud of giggling faeries surrounded him. Without a word, they latched onto his arms and legs and flew him up the long winding staircase. Within minutes he was at the Wizard's door, laughing and breathless after the unexpected flight. The faeries quietly set him on the stone floor and zipped back down the stairs.

Just as he was about to knock on the door, it swung

open. The room inside was bright. Andy could feel power pulsing from the illuminated crystal. The Gemstone Wizard stood straight and strong. His grey robe had turned into a long silvery gown and cape. His long white hair and beard gleamed and his merry eyes sparkled with delight.

"Job well done, lad. You've saved Dreamland. Through your determination and unselfishness, you have rescued our people from an unknown evil. Please accept my thank you on behalf of all of us." The Wizard bowed.

"You're ...... welcome," said Andy shyly. Surprised that his actions had such an immediate and extraordinary impact, he found himself speechless.

"Is there anything I can do for you, in return?"

"Uh, well... I really need to be getting home."

More than anything he wanted Tobee to be alive. But he felt foolish to request such an impossible task from the Wizard. And he *did* need to get back to his world. He had enjoyed the adventures here. Well, most of them. But he missed his mom and Brian.

"Of course, of course," the Wizard agreed. "But we were hoping that you would join in a celebration before you left. I understand some friends of yours are on their way here. I'm sure they would like to say goodbye to you."

"Oh. Okay," Andy's eyes lit up. He saw no harm in waiting a few more hours. And he'd like to see the friends that he'd met along the way.

They were interrupted by a knock on the door. With a distracted wave of the Wizard's hand, the door swung open. A trio of elves was at the door with questions about the party. While the Wizard gave them instructions, Andy wandered over to where the crystal ball sat on the table. The same table where he had left Tobee's body. Besides the crystal ball, the table was empty. Tobee's body was gone.

Andy's sadness resurfaced. He turned his back to the Wizard and the elves to hide his tears.

Slowly, he moved to a window and looked out at the surrounding countryside. The land was beautiful. It was such a different sight than when he had arrived. The meadow surrounding the castle was green and lush. Creatures of all shapes and sizes were arriving by land and sky. A buzz of excitement was in the air.

But Andy couldn't appreciate it. He closed his eyes and sighed. A tear fell and hit the window sill. When the next tear dropped, he jumped back in surprise. A tiny, indignant voice had piped up from the shadows.

"Hey watch it, ya big goof! You're gonna drown me!"

"TOBEE!"

The tiny faerie was sitting on the ledge. He was bright eyed and healthy looking. His wings were still darkened from the fire beating they'd taken, but were whole again. His clothes were torn and tattered and now wet from Andy's tear. Andy scooped up the faerie's tiny body and danced a jig. Now the tears really started.

"Tobee, I'm so happy you're okay. I thought you were dead."

"Naw. Ya can't get rid of me that easily."

"I'm so sorry you got hurt. I should never have let you fly out there…." Andy's blubbering apologies were interrupted by Tobee's guffaw.

"Andy, it's not your fault. Something had to be done. That monster was going to fry both of us, *and* the last Thunderegg. Besides, what makes you think you could have stopped me, huh?" Tobee thrust out his tiny chin and puffed out his chest.

They flew down the long spiral staircase and picked

their way through the increasing crowd that was gathering in the castle. Once they were outside the castle walls, they slowed down. It was a relief to be in the relative quiet of the meadow. Every once in a while a large bird would arrive bearing passengers. Horses and unicorns would step out of the woods with their backs loaded with riders. They all headed towards the castle. One unicorn veered off course and headed towards the boys. Two small blobs clung to its back. Andy, head cocked to one side, didn't recognize the slim muscular frog sitting in the front.

"Hey kid. How's it going?"

"Ziggy!" Andy gasped. He jumped to his feet. "What happened to you? You're not fa.... I mean .... You look great..." he finished lamely.

"Thanks. Woke up in this handsome bod," he stroked his chest. "And met this little lady along the way," he motioned behind him at the demur frog lady sitting behind him. "Pretty little thing, don't ya think?" he whispered behind his hand and wiggled his eyebrows up and down.

After introductions and a brief chat, the frogs and their unicorn taxi headed off towards the castle.

The boys lounged in the tall, lush grass and soaked up the sun's rays. A strange yet familiar thumping sound gradually grew louder. Confusion danced across both boys faces as they tried to place the sound. Realization hit them at the same time. They gasped and jumped to their feet. Tobee landed on Andy's shoulder and tried to hide under his hair.

"It can't be," whispered Andy.

Chapter 17

Out from behind the forest flew a huge dragon. It skimmed the tops of the trees in a lopsided, uncontrolled glide. As it approached the edge of the forest and the meadow, it sunk onto the tops of the trees. Loud snaps filled the air as tree tops were broken. As the creature sunk further down into the forest, the boys covered their ears. It sounded like a bulldozer was crashing through the woods. Whole trees toppled to the ground as the dragon finally emerged from the forest. The crashing and snapping continued on for several minutes. Finally, the dragon came to rest at the edge of the meadow.

Andy and Tobee watched in bug eyed silence as it hauled itself to its feet and headed toward the castle in a rambling walk. The ground shook at each step. The boys, cowering on the ground, were directly in its path. When it spotted them, the dragon stopped and lowered its huge head down to their height.

"Hey guyth. Whatcha doin'?"

"S-s-spike?" whispered Tobee.

"Yeah, who elth would it be?" demanded Spike.

Andy and Tobee stared, mouths agape. Spike was no longer the goofy little dragon wannabe. His huge, sleek, green body towered above them. Sunlight flashed and sparkled off his iridescent back. Large, filmy wings folded neatly against his sides. His ears, once huge, were in proportion to his body. A long, tapered tail trailed off into the grass.

"When did you get so big?" Andy looked up into Spike's golden eyes.

"I dunno. Latht night, I gueth. Thomthing happened. Hey, look at my wingth!" He spun around to show them his unfolding wings. In doing so, he almost knocked them over – first with his wing tip, then with his long powerful tail.

"Oh, thorry!" he exclaimed when he heard their screams.

"I'm thtill trying ta get uthed to everything!"

Andy and Tobee gave him a couple of weak smiles.

"Oh, and gueth what? I can breathe fire! I'm tho ex-thited! I already burned a tree outthide my houth. Here let me thow you." He took a deep breath.

The boys screamed. Andy shrunk to the ground. Tobee hid under his friend's body.

Spike let his breath out slowly.

"What?" he asked in confusion.

"Can you show us later. Please," whispered Andy as he cupped Tobee protectively in his hands.

Spike bent down from his great height and had a closer look at Tobee. He took in the faerie's tattered and burnt clothes. When his eyes passed over Tobee's darkened wings, he said, "Okayyyy. What happened to you guyth?"

The boys quickly told Spike their story.

"Geeth. I thought I wath the only dragon around here. Who the heck wath he?" Spike asked indignantly.

"I dunno, but he's gone now," Tobee said confidently.

"Andy threw him into a hole."

"Ahhh, Tobee. It wasn't like that."

Keeping in tune with his short attention span, Spike changed the subject. "Tho, Tobee, thinth you can fly, maybe you can give me a flying lethon? I think I need a little help."

Without waiting for an answer, the dragon clambered to his feet. As both boys started to protest, Spike's head drooped and if it's possible for a dragon to pout, then that's what he did.

"Oh boy," groaned Andy.

"It's okay. I'll give him some tips. I teach all the young ones back home how to fly," Tobee tried to sound confident.

"Okay, Tobee. You go right ahead. I'll be right here when you get back." Andy took a few backwards steps.

"Oh, no, no, no. You've gotta come with me, Andy. There's no way I'm doing this by myself."

Andy's shoulders slumped and he closed his eyes, groaning in resignation.

The next challenge was trying to figure out a way for the boys to stay seated on Spike's back during the flight. Andy and Spike were discussing different ideas when they realized that Tobee had disappeared. They searched the meadow and finally found him in a stand of long grass. He was a blur of green as he zipped up and down grass blades and then zoomed busily along the ground. Andy and Spike looked at each other in confusion and shrugged. All of a sudden Tobee was in front of Andy's face.

"Ready, Andy?" Tobee gasped, out of breath and flushed from his mysterious actions.

Andy didn't have time to respond before he plummeted to the ground, faerie size once again.

"TOBEE!" Andy bellowed.

"Yeah. Whatever. Here, hang on to these." Tobee ignored Andy's scolding and tossed a huge bundle of braided grass blades at Andy.

"Huh?" Andy, confused, gathered the rope into his arms.

"Okay, hang on," shouted Tobee.

In a blink of an eye, Andy was human size again. The grass rope had grown with him. He toppled over with the weight of it.

"Aw, geez," Andy groaned weakly.

"Hah! You're a geniuth!" shouted Spike.

Tobee, hands on hips and a triumphant grin on his face, looked at Andy and said, "Well? Whenever you're ready…"

Andy sat on Spike's back at the base of his neck - just in front of the filmy wings. The rope fit comfortably around the dragon's powerful neck. Andy hooked his legs under it and gripped the knotted ends. Tobee climbed under Andy's hoodie so his head peaked out over the collar.

Andy started squirming and giggling. He grabbed hold of Tobee through the fabric of his sweater and pulled him away from his body.

"Whoa," cried Tobee. "What are you doing?"

"Your wings are tickling me," gasped Andy between giggles.

"Oh, sorry," mumbled Tobee as he wiggled around so his wings were tucked into his back.

When Andy finally got his giggles under control and Tobee found a comfortable spot, they gave Spike the thumb's up. The enthusiastic dragon took off at a flapping run.

Andy and Tobee gritted their teeth as they were jostled back and forth. Then back and forth and up and down. Spike's huge wings flapped vigorously but unevenly. The ride was more gut wrenching than any carnival ride Andy had ever been on. Finally, Spike's feet left the ground and they were airborne. They skimmed the tops of the trees on the other side of the meadow as Spike's wings kept up an energetic beat. But his wings were flapping so unevenly, the boys thought they would be tipped off his back. Andy frantically bellowed Tobee's directions to Spike of how to even out his movements. When he finally figured it out and they were flying level, there was a huge sigh of relief from the passengers.

"Awthome!" exclaimed Spike. "Thith ith tho cool!"

They circled the Wizard's Castle where the celebration was in full force. The partygoers in the courtyard stopped and waved as they flew overhead. As Spike looked down to have a better look, his body started a nose dive. The shocked creatures below scattered. Some ran into the castle while others hid along the castle walls. Andy and Tobee yelled, "LOOK UP! LOOK UP!" until Spike got himself under control and they leveled off just in time to soar over the castle wall.

Tobee kept up a steady stream of instructions - hoping that in keeping Spike's attention on flying he wouldn't get distracted. Spike was a quick learner, although tended to over exaggerate movements with his enthusiasm.

Every ten minutes they kept hearing "Thith ith tho cool!" from the dragon.

They climbed higher and flew a lot faster than Kailani did. Mountains and forests whizzed underneath them. Lakes and rivers twinkled from a distance. As they approached another mountain top, Tobee instructed Spike to fly at a lower altitude.

"Hey, there's Kailani's tree," bellowed Andy.

Spike forgot lesson #1 of basic flying: *Don't look down.* They dropped through the air. Spike, realizing his mistake, looked up. He overcompensated and they ended up flying straight up. The boys, starting to feel nauseous with all the up and downing, groaned and rolled their eyes.

"Oopth, thorry guyth," apologized the sheepish dragon. He leveled off and began a slower, circular descent.

As they circled closer to the mountain top, Kailani's tree came back into view. Andy squinted and thought he could see her in the nest. As they came around again, closer, he saw her stand up and span out her wings in greeting. On the next trip around, they were even closer. Andy saw three small baby birds at her feet. Grey, with stubby feathers sprouting from their bodies and tiny curved beaks that mimicked their mother's, the tiny eagles stood up on wobbly legs. Spreading their almost non-existent wings, they comically copied Kailani before toppling over in a heap.

On the last circle around they were even with the nest. Kailani tucked in her wings, bowed majestically to Andy and gently settled her feathered body over her little ones.

The boys waved and hooted from Spike's back. They chattered with excitement as they headed back towards the castle. .

Spike was finally getting the hang of flying. They enjoyed a much smoother flight back. But they weren't there yet. Tobee silently worried about Spike's landing throughout the whole trip. Once he saw the meadow where the castle was, his heart flipped. After watching Spike's first landing he was prepared for the worst.

Below them a white horse gazed up at them from the meadow. It reared up and whinnied, galloping back and forth beneath them. When Andy and Tobee realized it was Boo, they hollered and waved with excitement.

Tobee made Spike circle the meadow several times as he attempted to explain the intricacies of a smooth landing. On their first attempt, Spike didn't slow down enough and had to climb up at the last minute to avoid crashing into the trees that surrounded the meadow. Below, Boo galloped full tilt into the protection of the castle walls.

Spike leveled off and circled again - ready to make another attempt. This time, he stuck out his belly as they touched down and dragged across the meadow. They stopped inches from the line of trees surrounding the field. Andy had closed his eyes long ago, his teeth bared in anticipation of a crash landing. Tobee, having given up yelling instructions, had burrowed deeper into Andy's sweater. When all was quiet and the dust settled, Andy hesitantly opened his eyes. Spike's eyes were squished shut, his quivering wings still at full span. His weight was balanced on his belly with his neck stretched straight out in front of him. His lips were pulled back showing his clenched teeth.

"Uh, Spike," Andy said in a soft voice.

"Yeah?" whispered Spike.

"It's okay. We're on the ground."

Spike opened his eyes one at a time. With a relieved groan, he relaxed and his limbs dropped to the ground, creating a cloud of dust and a minor earthquake. His long neck was stretched out, wings spread to both sides and his tail lay limp behind him.

Andy slumped, "Oh, man. That was wild."

Tobee climbed out of his hiding place and looked behind them. "Geez," he whispered.

A deep channel in the meadow showed the route where Spike's heavy body had dragged.

"Hey, Spike!" Tobee called.

"Yeah," mumbled the dragon.

"I think you're gonna need some practice on your landings."

"Ya think?" Spike's sarcastic answer made both boys chuckle.

Andy saw a flash of white out of the corner of his eye. He swung his head around and yelled, "BOO!"

He scrambled down from Spike's still prone body and dashed across the meadow towards the horse. She was approaching at a hesitant trot, staring wide eyed at the dragon.

Andy's enthusiastic greeting included hugging Boo's neck, petting her forehead and running circles around her. She snorted and nodded her head. Her large eyes and gentle knickers showed her pleasure and relief in seeing him again.

"Well, that was quite the show. Who's your friend?" She warily nodded towards the dragon who was watching them out of the corner of his eye.

"That's Spike. Yup, he's just learning how to fly. Can ya tell? Tobee was giving him lessons on the way. But there was no place to practice the landing."

Boo's head jerked up when she took a closer look at Tobee, who had settled on Andy's shoulder.

"What happened to you?" She asked with alarm when she saw his tattered and burned clothes.

"Weeeeell, we had a little run in with a dragon." Andy explained. "No, not Spike. A different dragon. In a cave," he quickly added as the whites of Boo's eyes flashed at Spike in fear.

"Riiiight. Okaaaay. You better tell me what happened." Boo sounded like a resigned parent who knew she was in for quite a story telling.

"Well, after we convinced Kailani…" Tobee started right into the story.

The boys took turns with the tale while they slowly made their way to the edge of the meadow where Spike still lay sprawled on the ground.

Chapter 18

Andy spent the afternoon lounging in the lush green grass with his friends. It took a while for Boo to get over her initial fear of Spike. They finally convinced her that he was not the dragon who had terrorized the land. He was such a likable young fellow it was hard NOT to grow fond of him.

As dusk slowly spread across the land, a group of tiny lights started to float across the meadow. A strong, bold light led the way.

"Hey, it's the King. No, wait. It's all of Faeritonia!" Tobee raced in circles around Andy.

"Come on, I'll shrink you. We'll get there faster if we fly," Tobee's voice was filled with excitement.

"Okay, but don't do it fast, Tobee. You should…ahhhhh… TOBEE!" In the blink of an eye Andy, the size of a faerie, lay flat on the ground.

Tobee snickered and danced away from Andy's reaching arms.

"You just wait. I'm going to get you. You rat!" Andy jumped up and started to chase Tobee into the tall grass of the meadow.

They played hide and seek for a few minutes until they were hopelessly lost. Tobee grabbed Andy's arm and they zoomed straight up and out of the grass. They spun in a circle until they spotted the approaching faeries. Giggling and chattering, they zipped off.

Boo rolled her eyes and went back to munching grass beside the dozing dragon.

It didn't take long before the moving mass of faerie lights veered away from their flight plan and zoomed towards Andy and Tobee. The boys were soon surrounded by an excited horde of faeries. There was such a commotion of greetings and endless questions that the King had to bellow for everyone to be quiet.

King Ferbinsol's voice was strong and commanding. There was no sign of his previous ill health and weakness. He wore his full royal costume, including crown and staff. A long green cape trailed behind him, floating in the breeze.

"Greetings, young men. It's good to see you both well and …intact," he looked them up and down and took in their tattered clothes and Tobee's burnt wings. "I'm sure you have quite a tale to tell." The crowd murmured in excitement at the prospect of a good story.

"But we'll wait until the celebrations begin."

The mob of fairies behind him moaned in unison.

"And I'm sure you'll want to clean up before we're all formally presented to the Wizard." Again the King looked them up and down with a critical eye.

He leaned towards Tobee and in a very loud whisper informed him that his mother would give him a hand. Tobee groaned and looked into the crowd. Sure enough there was his mother, arms crossed and a scowl on her face. The King patted him on his shoulder and chuckled as he continued his flight towards the castle. The rest of Faeritonia swarmed past. The boys were inundated with compliments and cheers and pats on their backs.

It wasn't long before they heard a high pitched voice

calling above all the greetings and hellos.

"Tobee. Where are you, boy? Tobee. Tobee! TOBEE!" From out of the crowd emerged Tobee's mother. As soon as she saw him, she stopped in mid flight.

"What happened to you? Look at your clothes. You come here this instant and tell me what happened to you," she demanded. She grabbed his sleeve and dragged him off, Andy trailing behind. Tobee glanced back at Andy with a sheepish and apologetic grin.

"Do you know how long it took me to make these clothes for you, Tobee? And they're your good set, too. I hope they have a needle and thread in that fancy castle. You better have a good explanation, young man…" The scolding died off as she scooted them towards the castle.

Chapter 19

The Wizard's castle was a beehive of activity. The faeries had an advantage as they were able to fly above the busy crowd. They settled on the mantle of the largest fireplace. Tobee and Andy were hauled off to a corner where Tobee's mother and oldest sisters did a very speedy clean up and repair job on their clothes.

By the time the boys were cleaned up, a huge feast was spread out on the tables filling the centre of the room. The Wizard made a long speech filled with gratitude towards Andy and all who had helped him. He was human size again so everyone could see and hear him. When he was asked to recount his adventures to the crowd, he broke into a sweat and started to shake. When he began his tale, his voice was quiet and he hesitated over his words. But he didn't stutter. The crowd oohed and aahed and gasped during the story. By the end of his tale, he was reliving the adventures with them and enjoying their reactions. Finally the cheers and applause were followed by the Wizard's order to 'Dig in!'

Everyone attacked their plates of food with relish. After Andy and Tobee were full, they sat back and watched in awe as Barry, who had joined them earlier in the evening, continued to eat.

"Wow, you sure can hold a lot," Andy mumbled.

"Uh huh," Barry replied. "My mom's always complaining how I eat too much, but I can't help it. I love food," he said the last with a bright smile and took another bite of a strawberry.

Hours later, with bellies protruding, the Dreamer and his friends were found lolling in a faerie sized hammock high up in a tree.

"Wow. That was great," Andy mumbled appreciatively.

"You got that right," yawned Barry. "I need to have a snooze before I go back for more dessert."

"I'm going to go see my ma. Make sure she's still not mad at me." Tobee dragged himself out of the hammock, leaving Andy and Barry swinging gently in the breeze.

Not far away, deep in the belly of the mountain, an angry and frustrated hiss could be heard echoing throughout the cave. No one heard it. Nor did anyone feel the sudden chill in the dark, dank recesses. The cave looked like a battle field with freshly burnt holes and streaks of soot sprinkled across the walls. Once scattered with randomly placed large boulders, the floor of the cave was a jumble of blackened rocks and grey dust. A pair of ominous red eyes spotted the trail of foot prints leading out of the cave and into the exit tunnel. The dragon's death hole, once empty and hollow, was now mysteriously filled with dark, still water.

Chapter 20

When Tobee returned, he found Andy and Barry sleeping. They were curled up together, slowly rocking back and forth. He snickered, then grabbed the hammock and shoved as hard as he could. Arms and legs and wings went flying as they were flung from their bed. The resulting screams and shouts bounced off the castle walls. Barry grabbed Andy's sleeve before he could plummet to the ground, then made a lunge at Tobee.

"Wait!" shouted the grinning faerie. His voice dropped to a whisper. "I snuck into the Wizard's room."

He pulled out a small woven bag. "I've got a surprise for you." Tobee whispered in a singsong voice while his eyebrows wiggled up and down at Andy. He thrust his hand into the bag and pulled out a handful of glittery powder.

Barry gasped as he realized what it was.

"Faerie dust? Tobee, you are in SO much trouble…"

Before he could finish, Tobee threw a handful of dust at Andy. Andy fell backwards in surprise and found himself falling through the air. He had fallen off the branch! He started yelling and flailing his arms. But nothing happened. He opened his eyes and found himself looking at Tobee and Barry. All three of them were hovering in the air.

"What?!" Andy's astonishment made the faeries break

out into a giggle. He spun in a circle, not believing that he was actually flying on his own.

"What happened? How is this happening?" Andy's eyes were huge. He didn't know whether to scream in fright or join his faerie friends in their snorting laughter.

"It's magic, ya goof!" exclaimed Tobee. "Tag, you're it!"

He slapped both of them on the arms and zoomed off into the trees. Andy and Barry looked at each other, grinned and whizzed off in pursuit. They played tag and hide and seek until dawn. Andy couldn't remember laughing so hard and for so long. He could fly! It was the most exhilarating feeling. He was a bit clumsy at first, but learned quickly. He had loved flying with Tobee – after he got over his fear of heights - but to be able to fly on his own was even more exciting.

When they grew tired of the game, they slowed down and made their way back to the castle. The closer they got, the more quiet they became. They knew that Andy would be leaving soon and none of them wanted to say goodbye. Along the way, creatures stopped their celebrating and said their farewells to Andy. King Ferbinsol thanked him again. Ziggy and his pretty frog lady ribbetted their farewells.

Silently, the boys arrived at the Wizard's door and sat on the top step.

Barry finally stirred and kicked at the air with his foot.

"Well, I guess I should go."

"Yeah," Andy reluctantly agreed.

Barry sighed. "Okay. Well, it's been fun." He looked Andy in the eye and flashed a sad smile, then turned and flitted back down the stairwell.

Andy, turning to Tobee, took a deep breath. "This

sucks."

They stood for a couple of minutes in silence. In unison, they turned and hugged each other. Just as quickly, they stepped back in embarrassment. Both boys started talking at the same time,

"I'll giantize you ..." began Tobee.

"You better make me..." started Andy.

They chuckled, then – whoomph – Andy was his normal size. He staggered backwards but caught himself before plummeting down the stairs.

"Whoa! I will never get used to that!" he giggled while Tobee snorted his laughter.

Andy stood up and dusted off his pants. Tobee flew up to his shoulder and they turned to stare at the door.

"Okay, I'm just gonna leave," started the faerie. "You have a good trip back. Don't forget us. And, well... I'll miss you." The last was mumbled as Tobee spun around in the air and zoomed back down the stairs.

Andy stood quietly, watching the tiny faerie light disappear around the corner.

The Wizard's door swung open as soon as Andy lifted his hand to knock. The Wizard didn't waste any time. Apparently, timing was important when returning Dreamers to their bodies. He started chanting and waving his hands over his crystal ball.

In a blink, Andy found himself in a quiet, grassy meadow that meandered between two mountain ranges. Boo was standing over him, her huge liquid eyes trained on his face. She nudged him gently – the equivalent of a horse hug, Andy thought. He smiled sadly and ran his fingers through her silky mane.

"I'm going to miss this place," he sighed. "Especially

the flying parts. And riding you, of course!" he added quickly. "Do you think I'll remember how to ride when I get back to my world?" he asked.

Boo thought for a minute. "I don't know if you'll remember anything. Maybe you'll remember it all, but think it was only a dream."

Boo kneeled down so Andy could climb onto her back. And then they were off. She set a fast pace, wanting to give Andy one last thrill before he left. The wind flew past, taking his breath away. He whooped and hollered, raising a fist in the air. The other hand gripped her mane. His body was bent over her neck, legs wrapped firmly around her belly. Boo's legs moved so fast they were a blur. She leaped over logs - a streak of white to anyone or anything that happened to be watching from the nearby forest.

Andy looked up and saw Spike swoop down towards them. He waved at the dragon as one of Spike's wings flapped up and down. This motion sent him floundering off into the distance. Horse and boy laughed in unison as Boo continued to cover the ground at lightening speed.

Soon, a wavering in the air to Andy's left caught his attention. He blinked. And blinked again. As he watched, the highway - complete with cars buzzing in both directions - slowly materialized.

"Wow!" he yelled.

He felt Boo chuckle underneath him.

As everything became more focused, they could start to hear the noises of a busy freeway. Andy looked frantically for his parent's car and whooped in delight when he saw it.

"There they are, Boo! Just ahead."

With one great effort, Boo leaped through the air in mid gallop and landed on the ground beside the moving car. She easily kept pace as they both peered across the ditch and into the car.

Andy's eyes widened in wonder. His mother was gesturing with her hands in an animated conversation with Brian. His stepfather was laughing and nodding his head. He looked at the back seat and saw his own head still leaning against the window.

"This is it, Andy," called Boo over the roar of the wind and sound of the highway. "You have a good life, kid."

Before Andy could say good bye, everything went black.

Chapter 21

Andy slowly woke to music and laughing. Without moving, he looked around and took a deep breath. His mom was telling Brian a funny story. The car radio was playing music in the background. He sat up and peered out the window. There was no horse. No faeries. No dragons. No fat frogs. Just the forest whizzing past them.

"Hey, you're awake." Brian winked at him through the rear view mirror. "I don't know how you can sleep through your mother's antics. She's a crazy woman!"

Andy's mom gave Brian a friendly punch in the shoulder before spinning around to greet Andy.

"Hey, mom." Andy's voice was groggy.

"Hey, you," she answered back softly. Her eyes took on that soft dreamy look that happened right before she told him she loved him. If she was close enough, he was sure she would plant one of her smooshy kisses on his cheek.

He was so glad to see her - he ducked his head to hide his tears.

"We're almost in Kelowna, honey. You slept the whole way. We couldn't even wake you when we stopped for gas."

Andy grinned at her and rubbed his eyes.

"Did you have a good dream?" she asked.

“Ohhh, yeah.”

“We got you a burger and fries at the last stop Andy. Want them?” asked Brian.

“Do I ever! Thanks … Dad.”

Brian gasped. His mom looked at Brian and blinked. She turned back to Andy and handed the food to him without taking her eyes from his face.

“Soooo, what would you like on it?” she asked slowly.

“Everything! I‘m starving. Do we have any ketchup for the fries? And is that pop for me, too? Man, I feel like I haven’t eaten in a week!”

Andy’s mom blinked. And blinked again. She kept staring at him as he ripped the paper wrapper off the burger and took a huge bite. Brian had turned down the music and was glancing at him in the mirror.

Finally, his mom asked, “Uh, Andy? Where’s your stutter?”

He gulped the mouthful of food down before answering.

“I dunno … I guess I must have left it in my dream.” He gave her a crooked smile and took another giant bite.

“Uh huh. Okay.” She answered softy. She slowly turned around and stared at Brian.

“Must have been one heck of a dream,” mumbled Brian.

“Uh huh,” was all she could say.

As Andy was finishing his meal, he glanced out the window. He stopped in mid gulp as he saw a shadowy, ghostlike figure galloping in the ditch beside the car. Just as he put his hand on the window and whispered, “BOO!” he heard a faint nicker.

“Oh! Did you hear that?” exclaimed his mom. “That was

a horse!" She peered out the window.

Andy strained to see, as well. But all he saw was the forest whizzing past. With a sigh, he settled back in his seat.

After he garbaged his meal remains, Andy rearranged himself to be more comfortable for the car ride. A hard lump in his pocket stopped his fidgeting. He reached in but pulled his hand back quickly. The scar on his wrist caught his attention. He rubbed a finger over the tiny wing shaped scar.

"Tobee," he whispered.

He grinned as memories of his faeirie friend flashed through his mind. Sighing, he dug into his pocket and pulled out ....the black velvet back with a piece of his Thunderegg in it. He had forgotten about it! The tiny piece of rock twinkled at him before fading to a dull green. Smiling, he rubbed it between his fingers. More memories of his dream adventure came flooding back.

His eyebrows shot up as he felt something wiggle in the pocket of his hoodie. When he thrust his hand in, there was a very tiny indignant squeak. Andy - bug eyed - slowly pulled out his hand. Nestled in his palm was Tobee.

Andy sat there, mouth agape.

"Hey," Tobee greeted him with a sheepish look.

"What?" Andy shook his head and blinked - not believing what he saw.

His mom spun around and faced him once again. "What was that, honey?" There were tears in her eyes, but she looked really happy.

Andy stuffed Tobee into his lap before she could see him.

"Uhhh, nothing," he mumbled. He shoved his hands further into his lap to smother the squeaks and curses coming from the squashed faerie.

When she turned back around, Andy bent over. He opened his hand to confront the squirming faerie.

“Tobee!?” Andy hissed. “How did you get here?”

Excerpt from Book Two

Andy's mom stopped in mid stride as she passed the kitchen counter. Eyebrows raised, she bent down to take a closer look at the cherry pie. A trail of tiny red dots covered the top of the pie crust, leading from the center hole to the outer edge. The hole was hollowed out with the crust sagging around the edges.

She stood up, confused.

"Brian!" she called.

He answered from the next room where he was reading the paper.

"What's going on with the pie?"

Silence. Then Brian's footsteps could be heard coming towards the kitchen.

"Pardon?" he came around the corner with a confused look on his face.

"Well, look." She pointed at the pie then looked at him with a knowing glint in her eye.

"Nope. That wasn't me," he held his hands up as if he could ward off her good natured scolding that was sure to come.

"Oh, come on, Brian," she crossed her arms and leaned against the counter. "Are you going to tell me another mouse has been visiting our pantry? Those are *not* mouse prints. Plus, a mouse would eat from the edge. Not methodically clean out the center of the pie."

"Honest, honey. I didn't touch it." Brian leaned over the counter to have a better look.

"Huh, looks like there's footprints going across the counter top," he mumbled.

"Andy!" his mom called out, giving up on Brian.

"Yeah?" Andy called from the balcony where he was reading a comic.

"Were you playing around with this pie?"

"Uh, oh," Andy straightened up and looked around him. Tobee was no where to be seen.

"TOBEE!" Andy whispered as loud as he could without being heard by the adults.

"Right here," answered a tiny voice.

Andy squatted by the potted plant in the corner and moved some leaves aside. Sure enough, there was Tobee lounging in the shade and picking his teeth with a toothpick.

Andy groaned and shook his head.

"Did you get into the cherry pie?" he whispered to the faerie.

"Awww, Andy. What makes you think that?" Tobee, trying to skirt around the subject without actually lying, sounded hurt - an innocent look on his face.

"Because you're *pink*," Andy hissed at him before spinning around and heading for the kitchen.

Sure enough, Tobee's head and arms were pink. He had tried to wash off the cherry pie syrup, but was left with a pink stain down both sleeves and on the front of his shirt. His hair was a sticky mess.

"Oops," Tobee muttered.

Go to www.ljlouden.com to find out what happens in Book Two of The Thunderegg Series.

Juan
Pablo